A
COMING
EVIL

A

COMING

EVIL

Vivian Vande Velde

Houghton Mifflin Company ▪ Boston 1998

The text of this book is set in 12-point Caslon 540.

Library of Congress Cataloging-in-Publication Data
Vande Velde, Vivian.
A coming evil / Vivian Vande Velde.
p. cm.
Summary: During the German occupation of France in 1940,
thirteen-year-old Lisette meets a ghost while living with her aunt who
harbors Jewish and Gypsy children in the French countryside.
ISBN 0-395-900012-3
[1. France — History — German occupation, 1940 – 1945
— Juvenile fiction. 2. World War, 1939 – 1945 — France
— Juvenile fiction. 3. Jews — France — Juvenile fiction.
4. Ghosts — Fiction.
I. Title.
PZ7.V2773Cm 1998
[Fic] — dc21 97-32196 CIP AC

Printed in the United States of America
BKP 10 9 8 7 6 5 4 3 2 1

To Bud and Elsie,
who always asked wonderful questions,
and to my mother, without whose help
I couldn't have written this.

PROLOGUE

Lisette Beaucaire was looking forward to turning thirteen. She was sure it would be the best year ever. Her mother's baby was due in March, and old Madame Champaux, who lived downstairs and knew all about such things, had declared definitely and repeatedly that it would be a girl. Lisette had wanted a baby sister for as long as she could remember. She even had a name picked out, Yvonne Hélène, though her parents had refused to commit themselves regarding this. Whatever the name, by January, Lisette was going through the chests where her mother had packed away all the lovely pink and lace dresses her aunts had made for her when she had been little. All on her own she cleaned and disinfected the baby buggy that had somehow survived cousin Cecile. Lisette enjoyed picturing herself and Yvonne heading to market or to church; the sophisticated and not easily impressed citizens of Paris would stare at them and ask each other, 'Who is that lovely thirteen-year-old young lady with the well-dressed baby?'

The best part about turning thirteen, however, would come in September, when Lisette would enter eighth grade, with all the privileges and advantages that entailed. Eighth-grade girls at l'Ecole Louis Pasteur still had to wear their uniforms, of course, but at last the plaid hair bow could be thrown away. Not having to wear hair bows went a long way toward making someone look grown up. According to Brigitte's older sister — Brigitte was Lisette's absolutely best friend — the classes were more interesting, too. That was because this was the next-to-last year of compulsory education and the teachers were trying hard to convince everyone to continue their schooling at one of the lycées. Whether or not this was true, Lisette was looking forward to being in the group that contained the oldest, wisest, most sophisticated students, and to having the younger children look up to her.

But the year Lisette turned thirteen was 1940.

1940 was the year that changed everything for everybody in France, and nothing was ever the same again.

It was also the year that Lisette met a ghost.

1.

Sunday, September 1, 1940

When Lisette woke up on the morning of her birthday, she had the feeling that it was later than it should be. Not that the room was too bright — ever since war had been declared with Germany, everybody had to have blackout curtains so that lights would not reveal the cities at night. But Mimi, who was the world's laziest cat, was up already, washing herself on the blanket folded at the bottom of Lisette's bed. Lisette wiped the sleep from her eyes and squinted at the nightstand. The clock there said 8:05.

Oh, no, she thought, scrambling to sit up, *not again.* Her parents might have overslept. They would be late for church again, just as during the week Papa was

1

generally late for work every third or fourth day. It was becoming a habit these last several weeks, her parents sleeping through the ringing of the alarm clock because the baby had kept them up half the night.

Lisette got down on hands and knees to look for her slippers. Mimi decided this was too much excitement and promptly curled up for a nap. One slipper was under the bed, too far away to reach without a long stick. Lisette gave up since she didn't have one handy, and since there was no sign of the second slipper anyway.

She put on socks because the hallway floor was cold throughout the year. At least, she thought, this time the baby hadn't cried loud enough to keep her up.

But then she realized that she could hear talking from the kitchen. So they weren't asleep after all. She supposed it was too much to expect that her parents had decided they could stay home from Mass in honor of her birthday.

Lisette peeked into the baby's room. Asleep, of course. Yvonne Hélène Beaucaire was like a vampire: she slept during the day, only to terrorize normal folk once the sun set.

Except that *she* was a *he.*

And his name was François Mathieu.

Lisette thought François was a terrible name for a baby, though Maman pointed out that he wouldn't be a baby forever. Lisette also thought that François was a terrible baby, but she knew better than to say that.

He didn't look like the pink, round, contentedly cooing babies in magazines. He was red and wrinkled and he cried nearly all the time. And when he wasn't crying, he was sleeping, and that meant Maman was constantly telling Lisette to speak, play, and move more quietly.

All in all, François was a bitter disappointment, and Lisette always thought of him simply as "the baby."

But if the baby wasn't the cause for her parents' not getting her up in time, what *was* going on?

In the kitchen, Maman and Papa were still in their robes. Maman had been warming milk on the stove — Lisette could smell that she'd scalded it — but now the gas was turned off, the pot apparently forgotten, the bread on the cutting board unsliced. As soon as Lisette entered the room, Maman and Papa stopped talking, so abruptly that she knew they'd been talking about her.

"What's happened?" Lisette asked as she walked around the table to sit next to Papa.

Papa motioned for her to share his chair, and he put his arms around her. Perhaps he thought she was cold in her nightgown. But she noticed with surprise that he was the one shivering. "We have decided," he said into her hair, "your mother and I, that it would be best for you to spend some time with your Aunt Josephine in Sibourne."

Lisette winced. "With Cecile?" she asked. Just as she always thought of her new brother as "the baby," she always thought of Cecile as "wretched cousin Cecile."

"Of course with Cecile," Maman answered.

"But this is the last full week before school." Lisette saw the look her parents exchanged and interrupted herself with an awful thought. "How much time will I be spending in Sibourne?" she asked, worry giving her voice an abrupt edge that she had not intended.

Neither of her parents said anything about little girls with bad manners, which was an ominous sign, and neither would look directly at her. "We're not sure," Papa said. "Just until things settle down in Paris."

"But what about school?" Lisette protested.

"There's a school in Sibourne," Maman told her.

"But I won't know anybody there and —"

"Lisette," Maman said firmly, then, taking away Lisette's last frantic hope — that for some unknown reason Aunt Josephine might say no — Maman added, "It's all been decided. You have just enough time to pack."

"Papa —" Lisette started, for her father would sometimes give in when her mother would not.

"Lisette," her mother repeated, even more firmly.

"Why?" Lisette demanded anyway. "Why do I have to go?"

Papa hugged her. "It will be safer away from Paris. With all the Germans here —"

She squirmed out of his arms. "You said it'd be safe

in Paris," she reminded her parents. "You said their tanks were made of plywood and the Allies would stop them long before they got here." That was in May, when the Germans had first marched into France. By the end of June, there were German tanks in Paris, and they were *not* made of plywood. The French government had fled south, leaving the Germans in charge of the north, with Paris as their headquarters.

"Lisette, don't talk back," Maman snapped.

The Germans weren't that bad, Lisette thought. Brigitte had claimed that they would prohibit the speaking of French, and that anyone who didn't understand German wouldn't be allowed to say anything but would have to communicate by grunts and gestures. That hadn't happened. Lisette's history professor had predicted that the Germans would loot the cathedrals and museums, and that hadn't happened either. Or at least it hadn't happened yet.

But there were Germans everywhere, with their crisp uniforms and their stern faces and their demands for identity papers and curfews, and there were terrible food shortages. Even in summer, which had always been a time of wonderful fresh fruits and vegetables, there wasn't enough. And this was what her mother used against her now. "There will be more food there, since they live in the country," she told Lisette, "and it will be safer."

In the other room, the baby began to whimper. Lisette looked directly at Maman. "Then will you be sending *him* also?"

Papa answered. "François needs Maman's milk, of course."

"Well, then," — Lisette turned to face him — "why can't we all go?"

Maman answered, as though it were a game for the one not asked to answer. "Because Papa is a pharmacist and so the Germans won't let him leave."

"Well, then," Lisette demanded, close to angry tears, "why did you wait until the last minute to tell me, so that I don't even have time to say good-bye to Brigitte?"

"So that we wouldn't have to listen to endless arguments," Maman said, and with that she turned her back on Lisette to go fetch the baby.

She's angry with me, Lisette thought as she packed, noticing how her mother's lips were drawn thin and the way she wouldn't look directly at her. *She's angry at me because of how I came home from Brigitte's house so late last Saturday, and now she's sending me away.*

I should have been suspicious, she chided herself, *the way they kept talking this past week about fresh country air and sunshine.*

She watched as Papa bounced the baby up and down to keep it from crying. They both liked the baby better than they liked her. "Little children, little problems," she had heard Madame Champaux tell her mother Saturday night; "big children, big problems." And Maman had agreed.

They packed all her clothes: everything, even her

winter coat and rain boots, proof — if she needed it — that they were in no hurry to get her back.

Lisette was determined not to ask. But as the taxi that was to take her and Papa to the train station stood outside, beeping its horn, Maman gave her a hug. "I love you," she said. "We'll send for you as soon as it's safer."

For a moment Lisette thought that Maman might be about to cry, that she *might* in fact have been sorry to see her go. But then the baby started to fuss and Maman hurriedly turned away.

Gasoline was so precious that the only cars permitted were German military vehicles, so the taxi was a taxi-bicycle, the back half of a taxi attached to a bicycle. Lisette felt sorry for the poor man pedaling, but she felt sorrier for herself. She and Papa rode silently down empty streets, past buildings draped with swastika banners. The last Lisette saw of her own house was her cat, Mimi, lying on the windowsill.

2.

Sunday, September 1, 1940

On the train Lisette and Papa shared a coach with another family: a mother — a beautiful dark-haired woman in an elegant dress; a father, who nodded politely to Papa and to her, then unfolded a newspaper and never looked up again; two little girls, both younger than Lisette; and a grandfather, who fell asleep before the train pulled out of the station and who snored continually.

Obviously, Lisette thought to herself, *obviously no one from this family is being sent off alone.*

It was going to be a long, long ride to Sibourne.

■   ■   ■

During the stop at Tours, not quite halfway to Sibourne, German soldiers got on the train.

Lisette could see them on the platform, going into the various cars. She expected the train would start up again immediately as it had at all the other stations, but they continued just to sit there. Some of the soldiers had remained on the platform, positioned — Lisette suddenly realized — to watch the doors of all the cars, to make sure nobody tried to leave.

The other family's mother had been reading a book to her daughters, but she'd been reading it loud enough for Lisette to hear — intentionally so, Lisette could tell by the way she'd look up and smile while turning a page. The story was too young for Lisette, but she appreciated the diversion anyway. Now the woman closed the book and leaned over to shake the grandfather awake.

Three Germans came into their coach.

"Papers," one demanded, speaking French after all.

One of the others started looking through their luggage. The third man said and did nothing. Apparently his job was simply to stand there and look menacing.

"What are all these books?" the second soldier asked.

"School books," Papa explained. "My daughter is going to be spending some months at my sister's farm, outside of Sibourne" — he winced as the man held up

Lisette's mathematics book by the covers and shook it with the pages hanging down — "That's arithmetic, history there on the floor, grammar still in the bag."

The soldier gave him an ill-tempered look, as though suspecting he was somehow being made fun of. He poked at Lisette's clothing, including her spare brassiere, which was lying on top of her panties. She felt her cheeks go red.

"Sibourne is on the border of the unoccupied zone," said the one who was holding their identification papers and travel permits. He sounded convinced that they were going to try something illegal. "What's this sister's name?" he asked. *"You!"*

Lisette jumped, realizing he was addressing her.

"You answer."

"Josephine LePage," Lisette said.

"And how old are you?"

"Thirteen."

"Birthday?"

Lisette squirmed. "Today. September first."

He was checking to make sure her answers matched those on her papers. Then he smiled, which did nothing to make him look friendlier. "Happy birthday," he told her.

She didn't have any answer for that.

He handed the papers back to her father and turned to the other family.

The other father handed over their papers.

The soldier didn't ask them any questions.

"*Juden*," he said to his compatriots. Then, to the family, "You will come with us."

"We have done nothing," the grandfather said. It was the first time Lisette heard him say anything. The voice was low and firm and had a slight accent.

The soldier folded the family's identification papers away into his own pocket. "It will be easiest for everyone if you come along quietly," he said. He took the arm of the younger of the two girls and pulled her up.

The girl looked from the soldier to her mother as though trying to decide whether to be frightened. The mother swept to her feet, bringing the older girl with her. More slowly, the father and the grandfather stood. Two of the German soldiers marched them out. The last, the one who had looked through their suitcases, stayed only long enough to open the window and toss the family's luggage out onto the platform.

Now that Lisette looked, she could see other piles of suitcases under other windows. There was a whole group of people, maybe two dozen, standing in a huddle surrounded by German soldiers. The family from their coach was brought there, too, then a single young man from another car. Jews, she realized. *Juden* meant Jews. Everybody knew the Germans didn't like Jews.

One of the soldiers must have given a signal, for the train blew its whistle and a few seconds later jerked into motion.

Papa leaned over her to pull the window shut. By

the time he sat back down, the train had moved beyond the station, leaving the platform behind. He put his arm around her, and it was only from his holding her that she realized she was shaking.

"What are they going to do to them?" she asked.

"Put them into work camps," Papa said. "They'll be all right."

"They weren't doing anything wrong. They weren't hurting anyone."

"I know," he said. And again he assured her, "They'll be all right."

But it took a long time for her shaking to stop.

3.

U ncle Raymond was with the Free French Army somewhere in England or the unoccupied south — at least that's what everyone hoped, for he had not been heard from since May — so Aunt Josephine had arranged for Lisette and her father to be picked up at the train station in Bordeaux by a neighbor. The man introduced himself as Maurice — Lisette wasn't sure if it was his first name or his last — and he was driving a horse-drawn cart. Maurice looked to be at least a hundred years old, but his horse looked even older. This turned out to be a lucky thing, for the cart seat was wooden and unpadded and if they'd been going any faster, the ride would have felt even more like a spanking.

They drove past miles of fields, though most of the fruits and vegetables were being sent to Germany. The countryside was very hilly, and by the time they pulled up the long driveway, full of weeds and holes, Lisette had decided that it was riding in the cart that had made Maurice look so old.

Maurice had a bicycle horn mounted on the seat next to him and he started honking at the foot of the driveway and kept it up until they reached the top, up behind the house.

Aunt Josephine came running out to hug Lisette and her father both. "Oh, Lisette, you've grown so tall since last summer," she said as Lisette climbed stiffly down. "And you won't believe how grown-up Cecile is since the last time you saw her. She's been so eager to have you here. She's been asking about you all day."

That was exactly what Lisette had been dreading, but she smiled politely.

"Maurice," Aunt Josephine called, "come in the house. I still have enough coffee to make us each a cup."

"I'll just stay here and read the paper," Maurice said. But he took out his pocket watch as a reminder to Papa that he only had a few minutes before they'd have to go back to the station so Papa could catch the return train to Paris.

As soon as Lisette crossed the threshold, ten-year-old Cecile threw her arms around her and practically knocked her over. "Lisette! Lisette! Come and read to me," Cecile began chanting.

"Cecile," Aunt Josephine said, "say hello to Uncle Arnaud."

"Hello, Uncle Arnaud," Cecile said, never glancing at Papa but tugging on Lisette's sweater, pulling it all out of shape. "Lisette, come and read to me."

"Give her a chance to put her things away," Aunt Josephine said. "She'll have days and days to play with you later."

Lisette tried not to sigh. The handle of her suitcase hurt her hand, so she put the bag down. "Where will I be staying?" she asked. She had been to the farmhouse only once before; usually, she and her parents visited Aunt Josephine and Uncle Raymond at their apartment in Nice. But Nice was in the unoccupied zone, and people weren't allowed to cross the border. Still, she remembered that there were a lot of rooms here, and she hoped to get whichever one was at the farthest end of the house from Cecile's.

But, "With me!" Cecile squealed. "You'll be with me!"

Lisette assumed that was just wishful thinking on her cousin's part, but Aunt Josephine was nodding. "Yes, you'll be sharing Cecile's room. Won't that be a special treat?"

Lisette looked to her father for help. He knew how irritating Cecile could be; surely he would defend her.

But before Papa could say anything, a little girl of about three peeked around the corner from the kitchen. Her eyes were so dark, they were almost black, and she wore tiny little earrings. As soon as she saw Lisette and her father, she ducked away.

"It's all right," Aunt Josephine called after her. "We're coming in."

"Who was that?" Papa asked.

"I'm not sure," Aunt Josephine admitted. "One of the twins, Emma or Anne."

Which didn't clarify matters one bit.

"Emma," Cecile said. "Anne spilled milk on her dress this morning and now she smells awful, like throw-up. Come up to my room, Lisette."

Aunt Josephine said, "Let's go in the kitchen first and meet the others."

"Others?" Lisette said.

"Others?" Papa said.

In the kitchen there were five children. The one Lisette noticed first was a boy who looked no more than five, who had a gas mask pushed up on top of his head like an ugly, lopsided hat. At the moment he was busy trying to fit himself into one of the cupboards. He had already pushed several of the pots and pans out onto the floor, and now he kicked aside a colander.

"Etienne, stop that," Aunt Josephine said.

The boy took her command to mean nothing else should be removed, so he climbed into the cupboard over the remaining pots and pulled the door shut behind him.

The girl Lisette had seen earlier was sitting on the floor with another girl, who looked just like her but who did, indeed, smell awful. Both girls had pot lids on their heads.

"You know how you can tell Anne from Emma?" Cecile announced. "Anne cries if you make this face at her." Cecile rolled her eyes up so that only the whites showed, then pulled down on the skin beneath her eyes and stuck her tongue out.

One of the girls began to howl.

"Cecile!" Aunt Josephine said.

Cecile talked over Anne's noise. "And that's Louis Jerome, holding his sister, Rachel."

Louis Jerome looked seven or eight years old. He was holding what Lisette had taken for a baby doll, but as Anne continued to howl like an air raid siren, the baby woke up and began to scream also. *Wonderful,* Lisette thought. The one advantage she'd seen to leaving Paris was that there would be no babies. Now here there were five of them. Plus Cecile. Emma, the twin who wasn't yelling, started banging pots together and Etienne opened his cupboard to shout, "Quiet! Quiet! Too much noise!" He slammed the door shut then reopened it immediately to shout again for quiet. Then once more he slammed it shut. Open, shout, slam. Open, shout, slam.

Aunt Josephine clapped her hands, the way Lisette's teachers sometimes did to get everyone's attention. Lisette's teachers, however, never had a group like this.

It was Papa who took charge. He picked up baby

Rachel from Louis Jerome and began bouncing her. With his free hand, he took the pots away from Emma. The next time Etienne opened his cupboard, Papa wedged his foot in the door. "That's enough," he said. "Come out of there at once." Then he told Anne, "She's stopped making faces, now you can stop crying." It didn't work right away, but eventually, all five children were quiet once again.

Then Papa turned to Aunt Josephine. "What do you think you're doing?" he demanded of her.

Aunt Josephine put on the same stubborn look Cecile usually wore. She was the youngest of the Beaucaire family siblings and was used to getting her own way. "What do you mean?" she asked.

"These children are all Jewish, aren't they?" Papa asked.

"Nonsense," Aunt Josephine said. "Anne and Emma are Gypsies, not Jews. And they're *all* the children of various friends."

Papa's voice was almost a whisper. "Do you have any idea how dangerous this is?"

Aunt Josephine shrugged. "Louis Jerome, come take your sister."

Papa handed the baby to the young boy.

Cecile said to Lisette, "Will you read to me now? Or should I read to you?"

Aunt Josephine swept out of the kitchen. Papa followed her and so did Cecile, with Lisette hurrying to catch up. Lisette wasn't going to remain behind with all these children, even if she had to be with Cecile to get away from them.

"If the Germans find out —" Papa started.

Aunt Josephine interrupted, "Yes, I know. If the Germans find out. We've become afraid to do anything for fear the Germans will find out. Don't let the French fleet join the British or the Germans will occupy all of France instead of just the north. Don't fight back or the prisoners of war will be executed. Complain and your neighbors might suffer for it. I've seen enough of German tactics to understand."

"Josephine!" Papa said in exasperation.

"Arnaud!" she answered, sounding just as put out.

He shook his head.

Aunt Josephine said, "The Germans won't examine every single household. Arnaud, nobody knows about them, not even Maurice. Here they'll have food, and they'll stay out of the work camps."

Papa looked at Lisette.

"And it will be safer for her, too," Aunt Josephine said. "Between the German execution squads and the English bombing us while they're trying to hit the Germans, we'll be lucky if Paris is still standing by the end of all this."

Papa gave her one of his not-in-front-of-Lisette looks.

"It's up to you," Aunt Josephine said. "Leave her here or take her back to Paris, but I won't send the others away."

"How can you take care of all those children?" Papa demanded, just as Lisette began to wonder which had come first: her parents asking Aunt Josephine to take her, or Aunt Josephine offering.

But Aunt Josephine didn't mention her. She only said, "They're not that much trouble. And Cecile is a big help. She loves babies."

Eventually, after Maurice had begun honking the horn, Papa finally agreed. He kissed Lisette good-bye, told her to help Aunt Josephine with the children, and whispered into her ear not to let Cecile make her crazy. "Be careful," he told everyone. And then he was gone.

Cecile tugged on Lisette's sweater. "Do you want to put your things in my room?" she asked. "Then you can read to me."

Lisette wanted to be alone, to try to get rid of the empty feeling inside. But she followed Cecile up the stairs and down the hall. "Are those two little girls really Gypsies?" she asked.

Cecile nodded.

Lisette had never met any Gypsies. Once, on the way to school, she'd seen a wagon stopped under a bridge. Two Gypsy women wearing a multitude of long, bright-colored skirts were arguing with the police, who were trying to stop them from doing their laundry right there on the banks of the Seine in the middle of Paris. The women were yelling and waving their soapy hands and only occasionally using French.

That was the only time Lisette had ever seen Gypsies; all she'd ever heard of them was that they were dirty — which clearly wasn't true even if they didn't pick the best location to wash — and that Gypsy women told fortunes and Gypsy children begged. Obviously the twins she'd just seen were too young to do either.

In her room, Cecile opened the armoire and indicated the last two inches of the rod. "Maman made me clean out one whole drawer for you." She must have had seventeen others. But she said, "It was hard. I had to move my ballet outfits in with my party dresses. Don't I have a lot of nice clothes? Maman wouldn't let me wear my nicest things last time we went to visit your family. She said what's the use, since they'll only get cat hair on them. Do you still have your cat?"

"Yes," Lisette said.

"Your parents will probably have to eat it. Are you ready to read to me now?"

"No," Lisette said, "I'm going for a walk."

"I'll go with you," Cecile said. "We can go anywhere except on that hill past the barn that overlooks the field with the chrysanthemum farm."

"Why can't we go there?" Lisette asked.

"Well, we *can* go there," Cecile said, "but *I* won't because it's haunted."

"Oh," said Lisette. "That's too bad, because that's where I'm going."

4.

Sunday, September 1, 1940

"Maman!" Cecile wailed, clambering down the stairs. "Maman, Lisette is being mean to me!"

Lisette took the stairs at a run also and reached the lower hall a mere two steps behind her cousin.

Cecile headed for the kitchen, no doubt assuming that Lisette would follow to give her own version of the story. Cecile was a born tattletale and wouldn't have passed up the opportunity if their positions had been reversed. But Lisette veered off to the right and flew out the front door. Her white patent leather shoes were meant for looking stylish, not for running outdoors. Lisette could feel the stones and twigs and bumps in the ground through the thin soles, and she knew she'd never get the grass stains out. But for the moment she only worried about not slipping and falling.

Behind her, she heard Cecile shouting, "Lisette! Lisette! Maman says you have to play with me! Lisette!"

The last was an angry, frustrated, giving-up wail, which was a surprise. Lisette had been afraid that Cecile, wearing more sensible shoes, might actually be able to catch up despite her disadvantage of three-years-younger legs.

Lisette didn't dare look back since her best defense would have been, 'What? Cecile wanted to play? I couldn't hear her.' But, as she started up the hill, she had to go partway around the barn and she glimpsed Cecile at the edge of the lawn. Cecile had stopped, apparently when she realized that Lisette had been serious about her destination. "Lisette," she called, her voice faint because of the distance, "come back or the ghost will suck your brains out through your ear!"

Childish trick to get her to come back. And besides, Lisette didn't believe in ghosts.

The hill was steeper and taller than it had looked from below. And once Lisette reached the top, she realized that it was bigger, too. Big enough to get lost on. But then, Lisette got lost easily.

She didn't stay at the edge, where Cecile would be able to see her and might get up enough courage to join her and make more hateful remarks about Mimi becoming somebody's dinner. Instead, she went in among the trees.

If I walk in a straight line, I won't really get lost, Lisette thought. *And if I do get lost, well that's a good excuse to be away from Cecile.*

Lisette walked in a straight line and in about five minutes came to where the ground jutted out from one of the surrounding limestone cliffs. It was unclimbable without ropes and special training. Lisette followed the wall of stone until she came to the edge of the hill.

From here she could see the south part of the chrysanthemum field and another section where a different crop, some sort of long grassy grain, was growing. There was a sprawling house with an orange-tiled roof in the distance beyond the grain field, probably belonging to Maurice and his family. If he had a family. Lisette didn't know anything about him, except that he was returning Papa to the railway station and she might never get back to Paris again. Beyond the house she could catch occasional glimpses of glitter, where the Dordogne River played peekaboo among the surrounding hills.

She went back into the trees, except this time she didn't walk in a straight line but headed for the middle, where the trees grew close together. They stretched tall toward the sky, their trunks thick and gnarled and incredibly old.

When she estimated she was in the exact center of

the old woods, she stretched her arms out. "I hate this place!" she shouted, turning slowly to include everything. "I hate every centimeter of it! And nobody's going to eat my cat!" Then, more softly, "I want to go home."

It didn't help. If anything, she felt worse. She couldn't avoid Cecile for the next six months — and she estimated it would take at least six months for the war to end, even if the Americans joined in tomorrow. And what if they didn't join in — or what if they did and the Germans conquered them, also? Everyone said that wouldn't happen, but they'd said Paris was safe, too.

Lisette sat down on the ground with her knees drawn up close to her chest. Maybe thirteen years old wasn't that wonderful after all. Maybe there was an advantage to being a younger child and not knowing what was going on around you. But thinking of younger children reminded her of the Jewish family on the train, and once she thought of them, she couldn't get their faces out of her mind. She rested her head against her upraised knees and tried not to feel sorry for herself.

A cold breeze touched the back of her neck.

Which was odd, since her hair covered her neck.

Lisette straightened up. Slowly.

The icy touch was gone, but she had a strong sensation that someone was watching her. She turned around quickly.

Nothing.

Silly, she told herself. Anybody trying to sneak up behind her — and by "anybody," Lisette was thinking of Cecile — anybody would have given herself away for there were no paths up here and a great deal of undergrowth. She couldn't imagine Cecile getting this far without making a lot of noise. Little children tried to be sneaky, but they just weren't very good at it.

So then why did she suddenly feel sure that there was someone standing behind her?

She whipped around.

Nothing.

Except . . .

Except the possibility that one of the branches right at the edge of her sight had moved. Maybe.

Lisette scrambled to her feet and faced that area. "Stop it, Cecile," she demanded.

She hugged herself for warmth and realized that her nice sweater that she had been so worried about Cecile pulling out of shape now had leaves and twigs stuck to it. She tried to brush them away and left a dirty smudge. Her dress would need to be washed, and her white shoes were all scuffed and stained, too. She hadn't been here more than a half-hour and she'd already ruined her clothes. Cecile would be pouty and miserable about being left behind, and Aunt Josephine would be annoyed both about the clothes and about Cecile. Not off to a good start at all.

"I'm going back now, Cecile," Lisette said, although she didn't really believe that Cecile was watching her from the bushes. Nobody was.

She was stupid to let Cecile's brain-sucking ghost stories make her so jumpy.

She pushed her way through the branches, refusing to look back despite the prickly sensation between her shoulder blades. There was no reason to look back because there was nobody there. But she did let each branch go with a snap, just to discourage anybody from following too closely, just in case there was somebody following, even though she knew there wasn't.

That made her feel better for about fifteen minutes, until she realized that she was hopelessly lost.

5.

The hill was at least twice as broad as it was long, but Lisette had walked across the shortest part in five minutes. Even given that she was walking at half the speed because this section was overgrown with tree roots and prickly bushes and fallen branches from years gone by, surely she should have reached the edge by now.

All she had to do was keep walking in a straight line.

But it was hard to walk straight when she had to keep circling around trees and clumps of bushes; in fact, it was hard to tell what *was* straight when she could only catch occasional glimpses of the sun because the trees were so tall and the branches frequently intertwined.

Lisette took her sweater off. She considered tying it around her head to keep the bugs out of her hair, but she decided if she was going to die here of starvation and exposure, she didn't want the search party that eventually found her body to think she looked ridiculous.

Don't be silly, she told herself. *You can't die of starvation and exposure on a hill that's barely bigger than the ground floor at l'Ecole Louis Pasteur. Somebody's bound to find you before then.* But she didn't put the sweater on her head.

What people would find ridiculous was that she could have gotten herself lost in such a small area. They'd probably send ten-year-old Cecile to find her.

But then she remembered that Cecile wouldn't come here. Cecile believed the hill was haunted.

Lisette thought she caught a movement off to the left. "Who's there?" she demanded.

Nobody answered.

Lisette intentionally walked toward where she had seen the movement, to prove to herself that she could. The area was much too overgrown for anybody to have been there. Could she have glimpsed an animal? Possibly a bird, because the movement had been at eye level, and she didn't want to think about any animal that would stand that tall. *Silly*, she told herself. *If it's too overgrown for a person, it's too overgrown for an ani-*

mal. And there probably weren't any more dangerous animals in Sibourne than in Paris. So she stood looking into the thickest section of interwoven branches and called out, just to make herself feel brave, "Come out, come out, wherever you are!"

And there, not an arm's length away, she saw a face.

She gasped and took a quick step back.

It never occurred to her that it was anything besides a ghost because she could see right through him just the way that looking through a store window you can sometimes see both a reflection of the street and what's in the store itself. The ghost also took a quick step back, so that now a branch seemed to be growing in his transparent head and sticking out through his ear. Which was very disconcerting to Lisette, if not to the ghost.

But the ghost seemed at least as startled and afraid of her as she was startled and afraid of him. And then he made a quick sign of the cross. A Catholic ghost? Lisette put her hand over her heart, willing it to stop pounding so hard. Back in Paris, Brigitte always made her hold her breath when they passed a cemetery, saying that you didn't want to flaunt being alive in front of ghosts, who were notoriously jealous of the living. But this ghost didn't seem aware of her breathing or of the beating of her heart. In fact, whatever had killed him, he looked ready to die all over again of fright.

And he couldn't be any older than Lisette herself, which was more sad than scary. She found herself saying, "Don't be frightened. I won't hurt you."

That seemed to calm him a bit. He was a good-looking boy, with brown hair and brown eyes, wearing a baggy shirt that hung to his knees, skin-tight pants, and tall boots. Old-fashioned or just poor, she couldn't tell. How long did ghosts remain in one place, she wondered.

He seemed to be appraising her, too. He said something, except that no words came out. The poor boy must be mute as well as dead, except . . . except wouldn't a mute boy have exaggerated the movements of his mouth so that she could read his lips more easily?

"What?" she asked. And the fact that he looked surprised at her question made her add, "I can't hear you."

This time, he did exaggerate it. In addition, he gestured toward her, then indicated himself, then touched his fingertips first to his lips, then to his ear. Obviously he was asking: "You can't hear me?"

She shook her head. "Can *you* hear *me*?"

He nodded.

This was getting stranger all the time. But now that she was over being startled, he certainly didn't seem frightening at all. She put her hand out to shake his. "My name is Lisette Beaucaire."

He hesitated, looking from her face to her hand, seeming uncertain what was expected of him. He stepped forward, and she felt a cold draft when his hand passed through hers.

She took an instinctive step back at the same time

he did. She wrapped her arms around herself, tucking her right hand under her arm to warm it.

He said something that she couldn't understand.

"What?" she asked.

He repeated it, and still she didn't understand.

"Your name?" she asked, and he nodded. "Say it more slowly."

Not only did he say it more slowly, but he shortened it, concentrating on the first name.

"Jean something?"

He shook his head.

"Gerard?"

He smiled. He had a wonderful smile.

"Gerard," she repeated. "Last name?"

He shook his head, looking more amused than out of patience.

"Do you come from around here?" She had changed the wording of her question at the last second, to avoid asking where he lived.

Still, he frowned in concentration and took another step back. He had gone right through the outermost branches, which now blocked part of his face.

"I'm not from here," Lisette said. "I'm just visiting and I'm lost."

At least he didn't retreat any farther.

"Can you show me how to get down from this hill?"

He only hesitated a moment before indicating for her to follow him. Then he took off into a tree.

"Gerard!" she called.

He must have turned around while he was actually in the tree, for he came back.

"I can't go that way. Can we go around?"

He looked at her quizzically.

Walking around that particular clump of tree and surrounding bushes, she walked as nearly in the direction he had started as she could.

In another moment he stepped back in front of her. But he had that wary expression again as if not quite sure he should trust her. When he thought she wasn't looking, he made another sign of the cross.

From the way he would walk around perfectly clear patches of ground, holding his arm up as though to force his way through nonexistent branches, and from the way he'd sometimes look back to check her progress and blink as though finding it hard to believe his eyes, Lisette gathered that just as he couldn't see all the surroundings that were obvious to her, he could see obstacles she couldn't.

This is ridiculous, she thought as he casually walked through a willow, *following a ghost to who knows where*.

But when she circled around the willow, she found herself once again near the edge of the hill, and very close to where she had originally come up.

"There's my house," she said, pointing. "I mean, Aunt Josephine's."

From the look he gave her, he couldn't see that, either.

"Thank you," she said earnestly.

He gave that disarming smile again, touching fingers to lips as though to say "You're welcome."

"Will I see you again?" Surely a ghost didn't come into being merely to help a lost girl find her way home.

From down below, she heard Cecile's petulant, "Lisette, you're in trouble now."

She glanced down at her cousin, and by the time she looked back, Gerard was gone.

6.

Sunday, September 1, 1940

Lisette started down the slope slowly, but she found herself going faster and faster, unable to stop. Cecile, of course, wouldn't budge, though she had to see that she stood right in Lisette's path. If the collision didn't knock them both out, Cecile would be sure to tell Aunt Josephine that Lisette had intentionally run her down.

Lisette skidded to a stop barely a nose's length from Cecile.

Hands on hips and obviously pleased with herself, Cecile said, "I told."

Lisette swept her hair back off her shoulders. "I'm sure you did."

Cecile followed close on Lisette's heels as Lisette

35

entered the house, obviously determined not to let her out of sight again.

In the kitchen, Aunt Josephine looked up from peeling carrots at the sink. "That wasn't very nice," she said, "running off without Cecile, not helping to get dinner ready."

"I'm sorry," Lisette said. "I was exploring and didn't realize it was that late." Which addressed the second complaint, if not the first. And which left a perfect opening for telling about Gerard. But though she had made no conscious decision *not* to tell about him, she hadn't said anything to Cecile, and now, as the perfect opening passed, she didn't say anything to Aunt Josephine, either.

"It's not that late," Aunt Josephine explained, "but sometimes the gas and electricity go off at six o'clock, so we have to make sure we're ready."

Paris might be the Germans' French headquarters, but at least there was electricity more or less regularly, except when the English were bombing nearby. Lisette didn't point that out. Nor did she take her last chance to mention Gerard. She said, "Let me set the table," and started for the cupboard.

But Aunt Josephine said, "Your hands are filthy. Better clean up first."

Cecile was standing in the doorway, making faces and looking pleased with herself.

"Cecile," Aunt Josephine said, "you can help the children get ready."

And if she had seen the face Cecile made at that,

Lisette thought, she wouldn't go around telling people how much Cecile loved babies.

Lisette went running up the stairs as Louis Jerome was coming down. "Be careful," he told her. "Running on stairs is dangerous. What if you fell?"

"That's what banisters are for," Lisette told him.

"If you fell on the banister hard enough, it could break."

Lisette looked over the edge and gauged the distance down to the hall floor. "It's not that high."

"But," Louis Jerome said, "if the banister broke, and you fell through, you'd probably land on the broken piece. What if it punctured some vital organ? You'd die immediately."

Lisette gulped.

"Or, what if you were lucky, and it just went through your hand, or maybe your leg? Then Madame LePage would have to send Cecile to Monsieur Maurice, since she doesn't have a car to get you to the doctor. What if Monsieur Maurice isn't home, or what if the doctor isn't in the office? You might bleed to death, or what if gangrene sets in —"

"Louis Jerome," Lisette interrupted, "be quiet."

The boy didn't seem at all put out. If he always talked like that, no doubt he was used to people shutting him up. He pointed to the clock on the mantle and said, "It's already five forty-five. Madame LePage likes us to eat at five forty-five."

"I need to change," Lisette told him. "I'd be done by now if you hadn't stopped me."

"All right, but don't run on the stairs."

Lisette refrained from pushing him into the banister.

By the time she'd put on a clean dress and changed her shoes, in the hope that Aunt Josephine had been too busy earlier to have noticed how dirty she was, and by the time she'd brushed the twigs out of her hair and washed her hands and face, everybody was sitting at the table waiting for her. The only exception was baby Rachel, who was asleep in a bassinet at one end of the kitchen.

Lisette took her place in the empty chair next to one of the twins, she couldn't tell which. Across from them were Etienne, Louis Jerome, and the other twin, with Aunt Josephine at the head of the table and Cecile at the end. Etienne was once again wearing his gas mask, this time pulled down over his face. Still, everybody seemed to be ignoring him, so Lisette didn't say anything either.

Aunt Josephine said, "We're having chicken tonight in honor of Lisette joining us."

"Yay!" the twins cried, probably more for the chicken than for Lisette.

Lisette was pleased, too. The last meat she'd had in Paris had been horse.

As Aunt Josephine selected a piece of chicken, the little girl across the table asked Lisette, "Were there Germans outside?"

Lisette shook her head.

"There could have been," Louis Jerome protested. "They could have been hiding. What if they followed you here?"

Exasperated, Lisette asked, "Have you ever seen *anything* outside that made you think there were Germans nearby?"

"We're not allowed outside," Louis Jerome explained. "What if somebody saw us?"

Lisette had no answer for that. Fortunately, Aunt Josephine handed the platter to her then and said, "Lisette, can you help . . . um . . ."

"Anne," supplied the twin sitting across from them.

The one next to Lisette smiled shyly. "Which do you want?" Lisette asked her.

Anne tapped her finger against the breast, which was the piece Lisette had wanted. There was another breast, but that was on the bottom of the plate, so she put the breast on Anne's plate, even though it was probably too big a piece for her, and took a drumstick for herself. Then she handed the platter to Cecile.

"Lisette saw a ghost," Cecile explained on Lisette's behalf, which Lisette knew was purely a guess, for Cecile had certainly not dared get close enough to see anything. Cecile dug under the legs and wings to get to the remaining breast, dropping a thigh and the back onto the tablecloth in her struggles.

"Ghost?" Anne's lip began to tremble.

"Nonsense," Aunt Josephine said quickly and

decisively. Perhaps too quickly and decisively. "There's no such thing as ghosts." She began ladling potatoes onto the girls' plates.

But Lisette had been looking at her. *She knows*, she thought. *She's seen him too. But then why doesn't she admit it? Why doesn't she just assure the children that he isn't a scary ghost?* Out loud Lisette asked, as though it were the most ridiculous thing in the world, "Do you believe in ghosts, Cecile?"

"I've seen lots of them," Cecile said. But then she added, "One is a huge, hairy man with these big oozy sores —"

"Cecile!" Aunt Josephine said as Anne began to howl.

"And a big German helmet —"

"Since you have so much energy," Aunt Josephine told her, "you can do the dishes when we're finished. Anne, please stop that."

Cecile shot Lisette a venomous look as though somehow this was all her fault. She took out her frustration on Etienne. "You have to take off the gas mask," she told him, "or you don't get to eat."

"No," Etienne said, his voice muffled by the mask.

Cecile reached over him to hand the meat platter to Louis Jerome.

Etienne grabbed the plate, Louis Jerome tugged, Cecile wouldn't let go, and Anne poked Lisette, while Emma explained on her sister's behalf, "You didn't cut it. You're supposed to cut her meat for her."

Just then Aunt Josephine looked up. "Children, stop fighting over the chicken. There's enough for everybody."

Louis Jerome and Etienne simultaneously let go.

Cecile did not.

The platter flipped in her hand, and the remaining pieces of chicken went flying at Lisette and Anne. Lisette ducked, and the chicken sailed harmlessly over her head. But Anne jerked her chair back, yanking the tablecloth halfway across the table and sloshing the children's lemonade out of their glasses. Aunt Josephine slammed her hands down on the table to keep the cloth from coming off entirely and knocked over her glass of wine. Lisette caught her plate — face-down — on her lap. Across the table Emma gleefully clapped her hands. "Do it again!" she squealed.

Aunt Josephine gave her such a look that she only said it once.

Etienne dove under the table. "Don't panic, men," he yelled, "but we're under attack!"

Meanwhile, Rachel had started crying.

Lisette looked over and saw that one of the pieces of chicken had hit the bassinet and was now lying on the baby's chest.

At which point the lights flickered once, dimmed, then went out.

Lisette rested her head on her hand. *Welcome to Sibourne*, she told herself.

7.

Sunday, September 1, 1940 –
Monday, September 2, 1940

Lisette decided that the safest thing to do was to go to bed. She was sure she'd never actually be able to fall asleep, missing her parents despite herself, remembering things and wondering about what she'd seen that day. But the next thing she knew, Cecile was pulling back the heavy blackout drapes and letting in the morning sunshine.

At breakfast, just as everyone was finishing, Aunt Josephine suddenly pulled a pocket watch out of her apron pocket. Very calmly she announced, "German drill."

"What?" Lisette asked.

Aunt Josephine reached across the table to place her hand over Lisette's. "For this time, just watch."

Everybody else was moving — quickly but methodically. They all brought their dishes to the sink, then Louis Jerome picked up baby Rachel; Emma and Anne held hands; Etienne pulled his gas mask down over his face. As Cecile gathered up four of the seven placemats and tossed them into the linen closet, the other children headed for the basement door. They disappeared downstairs while Cecile went thundering up the stairs to the bedrooms.

Lisette's hands were clammy and she was having trouble sitting still. A *drill*, Aunt Josephine had said. And certainly she had never been afraid of fire drills at school. She was even getting used to the air raid sirens. But the idea that Aunt Josephine was worried about Germans was scarier than knowing that her parents were worried, for her parents worried about everything, and Aunt Josephine had always been as unorganized and unconcerned as any of the cousins in the Beaucaire family. But here she was *planning* for the possibility of Germans coming. Hadn't her parents sent her here specifically to be safe from the Germans?

At the point when they could no longer hear banging doors or running footsteps, Aunt Josephine checked her watch. "Forty-seven seconds," she said. "Not bad." She put the watch back in her apron pocket. "Let's check Cecile first."

Lisette had assumed Cecile had been heading for their room, but instead she was in the room Etienne and Louis Jerome shared, sitting on their unmade bed, playing with a doll.

"Vell, little girl," Aunt Josephine said in what was no doubt supposed to be a gruff German officer's voice, "vhat have ve here? This is your room?"

"No," Cecile said, in a prim and proper voice. "This is a spare bedroom. I'm just playing in here. This is my doll, Julie, and she's exploring caves." Cecile stuck her doll under the blanket and moved it around, as though that were how the sheets had gotten mussed.

Aunt Josephine opened some of the drawers. "And these clothes? These little boys' clothes?"

"They belong to my boy cousins from Tours. They visit often, and they leave some of their extra things here so they don't have to pack them and bring them on the train every time."

"Ve shall see, little girl," Aunt Josephine said, trying to sound ominous. "Now show me the other rooms."

Lisette found that her throat was tight and dry as Cecile led the way down the hall. *Calm down*, she told herself. If she got this flustered during a drill, she'd fall apart totally if Germans ever really came. But surely if Cecile could do it, so could she.

At the twins' room Cecile said, "This is the room I used to use. See all my baby things? Now I have the bigger room down at the end of the hall."

"This bed, too, is unmade," Aunt Josephine pointed out in her bad accent. "More explorations of the caves?"

"No," Cecile said. "My cousin Lisette is visiting from Paris. Normally she stays in my room, but last night we had a big fight, so she slept here."

Aunt Josephine forgot her German impersonation. "Very good," she said.

"Thank you," Cecile said in her everyday voice. "I just thought of that this morning." She pointed to the room across the hall that looked like an adult's except that it held Rachel's bassinet. Cecile pointed to the doll that lay among the blankets and continued in her formal tone. "And that's Lisette's dumb doll, Mimi." She stuck her tongue out at Lisette, and Lisette stuck hers out at Cecile. The joking helped. A little.

"So," Aunt Josephine said in her normal voice, "Lisette, if the Germans come during the night or early in the morning when the beds haven't been made yet . . ."

"Cecile and I can't stand each other" — that would certainly be easy enough to pretend — "and I'm in the room the girls share."

"It's the responsibility of whoever takes Rachel out of her bassinet to put a doll in her place so that the bassinet looks like a toy."

Lisette clicked her heels and saluted.

"Very good," Aunt Josephine said. "Now the basement."

When Lisette opened the basement door, there was no light. She felt around for the switch, but when she found it, it didn't work.

"The light bulb blew out yesterday," Cecile explained in her talking-to-Germans tone, "and Maman hasn't replaced it yet."

Aunt Josephine was rummaging around under the sink and finally brought out a flashlight. "If the Germans come when I'm not here, search all the other cupboards first," she said, "for the extra time it will give the children."

Lisette nodded. "But isn't it dangerous, the little ones running down the stairs in the dark?"

"They use the extra flashlight we keep here." Aunt Josephine indicated the space between the wall and the stairs. "I'll go first. Follow closely and be careful."

The stairs were wooden slats with no backs, but they were sturdy. And although the basement floor was packed dirt, the place was dry, not damp and musty like the basement of Lisette's family's apartment building in Paris. Aunt Josephine shone the flashlight in an arc that revealed a huge old furnace, wooden crates piled haphazardly against the walls, lawn furniture stacked away now that summer was gone, and probably half the world's supply of cobwebs.

There was no sign of the children.

"See if you can find them," Aunt Josephine said. She handed Lisette the flashlight.

Lisette checked around the crates. "Should I take these down?" She indicated some that blocked others in back. There was no telling what kind of bugs made their homes back there.

But Aunt Josephine was shaking her head. "We'll assume the Germans will, but don't bother."

There was a door off to the left. Cecile giggled, so Lisette guessed that probably she wasn't anywhere near the children, but she opened it anyway. It was a coal bin, less than half-full now, with a chute down which the coal was delivered and a wheelbarrow and shovel in the corner for bringing the coal to the furnace. Everything was thickly coated with black coal dust. In fact Lisette had some on her hand just from lifting the door latch. "Do I need to check under the coal?" she asked. She couldn't imagine Aunt Josephine hiding the children there and subjecting herself to all the laundry that would entail.

"Cold," Cecile said, "as cold as can be."

"Shh," Aunt Josephine said. "No hints." Then to Lisette, "But no, they're not in here."

There was another room that had racks and racks of wine bottles. Lisette walked all around the racks and shone the flashlight underneath, but the children weren't there either.

Other little rooms had shelves holding jars of homemade preserves and canned vegetables. There were burlap bags full of apples, turnips, and onions, though there were many more bags that were neatly folded and empty.

Lisette found what must have been Uncle Raymond's work area. Tools and a portable utility light with a long extension cord hung on the wall. On the dusty workbench lay a dismantled toaster. Would he ever return home to put it back together? she wondered. Or was he dead already, and nobody even knew it? *Stop it*, she told herself. The Germans would never come here, and Uncle Raymond was fine. She shone the flashlight under the workbench. Nobody there.

She returned to the clothes trunks, which she had already dismissed as being too small, and opened them. Off-season clothes packed in mothballs.

"I give up," she finally announced.

"Call them," Aunt Josephine said.

"Come out, come out, wherever you are," Lisette chanted before remembering that was what she'd said just before Gerard had appeared. But neither ghost nor children came. "Louis Jerome." She raised her voice. "Emma and Anne. The drill is over. Etienne." She looked at Aunt Josephine helplessly. The only thing that kept her from worrying that something had gone wrong was the smug smile on Cecile's face.

"Long live France!" Cecile called out.

Finally, Lisette could hear stirrings from the children.

"Long live France is the secret password," Cecile explained to Lisette. "It means everything really is fine and we're not just calling them out because the Germans are forcing us to."

The children emerged from the room where she'd

seen the burlap bags of fruits and vegetables.

"But . . ." Lisette protested, knowing there hadn't been room behind the filled bags nor beneath the empty ones.

"Look," Aunt Josephine said. Then, to the others, "Don't close the secret door behind you." She shone her flashlight on the far wall of shelves, which had swung in on unseen hinges. Behind the storeroom was a small second room, completely lined with heavy blackout curtains, even the dirt floor. "The curtains let the children keep the flashlight on so they don't have to be in the dark," Aunt Josephine explained.

They'd also help keep the room a bit warmer in the winter, Lisette thought, seeing the blankets that were piled in the corner. On a shelf there were also a jar of drinking water, a tin of powdered milk, and extra diapers. "It's a very good hiding place," she said. "Is there some sort of hidden lock to open the door?"

"No," Aunt Josephine said as though it were a ridiculous question. "You just push on any of the shelves."

Cecile demonstrated.

"It's not meant to be a secret room. There used to be a handle, but I took it off."

"It's very clever," Lisette said.

"Thank you," Aunt Josephine said. Then, with a sigh as they started up the stairs, she added, "I just hope we never have to use it."

Lisette fervently hoped not, too. But she had seen

the Germans march into Paris and she suspected the Germans generally got whatever they set their minds to.

8.

Aunt Josephine had plans for what to do no matter when the Germans might come. Always the first part of the plan was that the Jewish and Gypsy children were to go to the basement immediately, not to make a move, not to make a sound until Aunt Josephine, Cecile, or Lisette said "Long live France." The second part of each plan was that it was up to Aunt Josephine, Cecile, and Lisette to do what they could to hide the evidence of the extra children being in the house. Lisette had just seen what to do if the Germans came in the early morning before the beds were made. If the Germans came during the night, it was much the same, except that Aunt Josephine

51

would be shocked and annoyed to see the spare-room beds in such a state, and she would say something such as, "So that explains all the noise you two were making earlier."

If the Germans came during mealtime, that was the worst, because it meant throwing all the food into the garbage bin; and while there was more food available in Sibourne than in Paris, there certainly wasn't enough to throw away.

If the Germans came while the children's laundry was hanging up to dry, that was because Aunt Josephine was washing outgrown clothing from Cecile and the cousins from Tours before she donated it to the needy. Diapers were never to accumulate, since there was no explanation Aunt Josephine could think of for a dirty diaper. So, though they only boiled the diapers once a day, each diaper had to be thoroughly rinsed immediately so that they looked like cleaning rags.

Once school started for Lisette and Cecile the following week, Louis Jerome, being the next oldest, would be in charge while Aunt Josephine went to market in the morning. It would take her about two hours, bicycling to Sibourne and back. She explained that she couldn't wait until the girls came home because she had no reason for doing so that wouldn't arouse the shopkeepers' suspicions. Lisette decided that the children were probably safer with Louis Jerome than they were with Aunt Josephine, given his inclination to worry about every detail.

"All right," Aunt Josephine said, "we've gotten a late start today. Lisette and I will go marketing after lunch so I can show her around Sibourne. Meanwhile, Cecile and Lisette, you can make the beds. Louis Jerome, you will help me wash clothes. Etienne, fill the basket on the porch with peas, and Emma and Anne will shuck them for lunch."

"Why am I always the one who has to make the beds?" Cecile asked. Then, simultaneously, she and Louis Jerome said, "I want to shuck peas." Anne tugged on Aunt Josephine's skirt. "Wash," she demanded. (The way to tell the twins apart, Lisette had come to realize, was by listening rather than looking. Anne generally let Emma do the talking, so Emma sounded older than three, whereas Anne sounded younger.)

After about five minutes of trying to pair each child with a chore he or she not only wanted but could likely perform, punctuated by Anne's chanting, "Wash, wash, wash," Aunt Josephine's patience snapped. "No," she said. "You will all do what I told you at the beginning. Lisette . . ." She'd obviously forgotten what tasks she'd originally assigned to whom. "Lisette, take charge. Once everyone's finished, you may all play."

While Aunt Josephine went to get the washboard, Lisette gave Louis Jerome a gentle push in the direction of the bathroom, where they'd wash the clothes in the tub. "The rest of you," she said, " get on the porch and wait for Etienne to bring in the peas." She grabbed hold of Cecile's arm as Cecile went to follow. "You're helping me," she reminded.

"I know that," Cecile said. "I was just going to remind them not to make a mess."

"They'll remember," Lisette said. "And stop stomping your feet," she added as they went up to the bedrooms.

"I'm not stomping," Cecile said, stepping hard enough that each stair vibrated.

As they started making the first bed, Cecile tugged so hard on the sheets that she yanked them out of Lisette's hands. Then she shoved the sheets and blankets under the mattress without smoothing out the wrinkles and lumps. By the third bed, Lisette decided she'd get it done faster and better alone, and she ordered Cecile downstairs to help with the pea shucking.

Now how did she manage that? Lisette asked herself, realizing she'd just given Cecile permission to do what Cecile had wanted all along. But she didn't call Cecile back.

By the time she finished and went downstairs, the pea shucking was obviously over. She could hear Cecile in the front room, rattling a jigsaw puzzle box, refusing to put it down until everybody sat where she told them to. Lisette tiptoed past the doorway and out through the porch.

Outside, Aunt Josephine and Louis Jerome were hanging the laundry on the line, although Louis Jerome was spending less time helping than anxiously watching for approaching Germans. Baby Rachel was napping on a blanket in the shade of the laundry basket.

Someone, presumably Aunt Josephine, had set out a bowl with a few table scraps, and a lovely gray and white cat was eating from it. "I didn't know you had a cat," Lisette said, leaning to scratch it between the ears, which her own cat loved. "What's its —"

Before she could say "name," Aunt Josephine called, "Don't —" and the cat hissed and scratched Lisette's hand.

Lisette jumped back, the cat resumed eating, and Aunt Josephine came running to examine her hand.

"I'm sorry," Aunt Josephine said. "I should have warned you earlier. She's a stray we're trying to tame and she's rather nervous. Those are nasty scratches. You'd better wash them off."

Rather nervous? Lisette felt betrayed. She returned to the kitchen, where she turned the water on to a trickle so nobody would hear. The second time she went out, she made a wide circle around the cat.

Aunt Josephine waved, which Lisette took to mean that they didn't need any help, so she walked in a leisurely fashion in the other direction, toward the chrysanthemum field. Aunt Josephine and Uncle Raymond had never been serious farmers; they were city people with farmland. Before the war they had raised flowers in the summer for a little extra income, but this year's crop were leftovers from last year's seedlings. This spring Aunt Josephine had spent her time and energy planting and tending a vegetable garden, and the flowers were overgrown and wild. Lisette spent about thirty seconds looking and sniffing; then she took off at a run around the barn and up the hill.

"Gerard!" she called breathlessly once she made it to the top. Would she have to get lost again to find him? But the next moment he was standing there beside her. Now she felt foolish and tongue-tied. "Hello," she said in a much more subdued tone.

But he looked pleased to see her. He looked overjoyed. His mouth formed the words "Hello, Lisette," and he reached to take her hand. She was sure he meant to kiss it, but his fingers passed coldly through hers, and that sobered both of them.

"I wanted to thank you again," she said, "for helping me find my way."

He gave that wonderful smile of his and touched his hand to his heart. Apparently nothing could disconcert him for long. He was just a bit too charming to be entirely sincere, she thought, but that didn't make the smile any less appealing.

"Well," she said — *Why am I here?* she asked herself; *what did I expect from this meeting?* — "are you . . . all right here? *(Can a ghost be all right or not all right? Does he know he's a ghost?)* Is there anything you need?"

He answered something longer than yes or no that she couldn't understand, but he gave up after repeating it twice.

In the stories she and Brigitte had read together, ghosts haunted places because their spirits had to be set to rest, usually because of some injustice that required righting. She asked, "Do you need me to get something, or do something?"

The question was not what Gerard expected, she could tell. He looked bemused but took the time to consider — probably so that she wouldn't feel a total fool.

But she did anyway.

He shook his head and mouthed the word "No."

Without any details, she tried to speculate what all the possibilities could be. "Do you need me to tell people something?"

She understood his answer, "I don't think so" — she could read his lips for something that easy at least. But he suddenly stopped. His eyes widened, he took a deep breath — he *seemed* to take a deep breath — *He's a ghost, you idiot*, she reminded herself. "What?" she asked.

He made the sign of the cross, the first today. "Who are you?" she was sure he demanded. And then — she thought — "What do you want?"

Why was he suddenly so wary of her? "I'm Lisette Beaucaire. You know that already. You helped me, so I wanted to help you. It only seemed fair."

He asked something, and she had to have him repeat it. He added gestures this time, pointing to her, then indicating their surroundings. Most likely, "Why are you here?"

"My parents sent me here, to get away from the Nazis in Paris."

He looked at her blankly. It probably meant he was more than ten years dead, if he didn't know about Nazis.

"The Germans," she said.

Still he didn't understand. She remembered her history lessons and reevaluated. If he didn't know about the Great War with Germany, he was more than thirty years dead. If he'd *never heard* of Germans, he was older than she wanted to think about.

"War," she said.

That he understood.

"We're at war with the Germans, and my parents thought I'd be safer here."

He started to say something, changed his mind, reworded it, changed his mind again, and finally asked — she was sure because, of course, it was the only logical question — "What year is it?"

"1940," she told him.

Could ghosts pale? She was sure Gerard did. It wasn't that he became transparent or less solid. If anything, he seemed less see-through than the previous day. But his face went — Lisette suddenly understood the expression — ghostly white. He sank to his knees and covered his face.

Instinctively, Lisette reached out to touch his shoulder, but there was only the sensation of cold. She crouched down beside him. "I'm sorry," she said, not knowing what she was sorry for, except that she had hurt him.

He looked up at her, still obviously shaken.

She took a deep breath, and *she* asked *him* the only logical question, which was still: "What year is it?"

He took a steadying breath, but she couldn't make out his answer.

She brushed a clear spot on the dirt. "Write it," she said.

He gave his head a brusque shake, barely a twitch.

He didn't know how to write, Lisette realized. That pushed his time back even farther.

"Say it again more slowly," she told him. He did. "One thousand . . ." He nodded. "*Three?* hundred . . ." Again the affirmative. "Fourteen?"

She moved from her crouch to a sitting position. No wonder he'd had the breath knocked out of him. 1314. More than six hundred years ago. For some reason, his being a ghost was easier to imagine than that he had been alive six hundred years ago.

He once again rested his face in his hands.

From down below she heard Cecile's voice call, "Lisette! Maman says it's time to help with lunch!" Even from this distance she could tell by Cecile's tone that Cecile was stomping her feet. "Maman says *now*, Lisette!"

"I'll be down in a minute!" Lisette yelled back.

Gerard jerked upright, startled, and she went cold all over.

"You didn't hear her?" she asked. "Did you?"

And, as if she wasn't sure enough already, Gerard glanced the wrong way — back into the trees on the hill rather than down the slope — before cautiously shaking his head. "Hear?" she could see his mouth form. "Her?"

Lisette watched Cecile run toward the house. She was aware of Gerard following her gaze, then looking back at her. Why was this happening? *What* was happening?

"I have to go back," she said. "I'll try to come here again tomorrow." As an afterthought she added, "If you want."

This time he wasn't so quick on the charm. He hesitated a moment before inclining his head in a short bow and mouthing the word "Please."

Lisette stood — too abruptly, it turned out. Her right foot had gone to sleep and she pitched forward, right over the edge of the hill.

"Lisette!" Gerard cried, lunging forward to grasp her arm. His fingers passed through her like a chill just as she caught hold of an exposed tree root. She'd only slid down a few feet and was more dizzy from the fact that Gerard was standing on thin air a good two feet beyond the edge of the hill than from the tumble she'd just taken.

She scrambled back up to the top of the hill and motioned Gerard to get back onto solid ground.

He did, but he looked as queasy as she felt. "It

appeared the earth just swallowed thee up," he said.

"Yes," she said, concentrating on making sure her skirt was down all the way around because she had to do *some*thing with her hands. "Well. It looked to me as though you were standing in the air. And here's something else to consider: I can hear you."

"Thou can hear me?" he echoed. "For how long has this been?" He had a definite accent, and some of his sentences sounded stiff and old-fashioned.

"Starting from when you called my name just now."

He sighed. She could hear that, too, a definite exhaling of what certainly sounded like breath, and he crouched beside her. "Are thou injured?" He caught himself before touching the ankle she was massaging.

"I'm fine," she said.

Gerard looked from Lisette to the edge of the hill and back to her again.

"What do you see," Lisette asked, "when you look down there?"

"The ground extends" — he paused to calculate — "a spear length or so beyond thee. Then the hill slopes gently down. There are many trees." He shrugged. Unsure of what she wanted, he added, "Elms . . . maple . . ."

Whatever a spear length was, it was probably longer than the handbreadth she could see. "You don't see the farmhouse or the barn?"

Calmly, warily, he said, "No."

"The fields?"

"No."

"I have to go." Lisette got to her feet more slowly this time. Her foot felt tingly but it could support her weight.

"But —" Gerard said.

"I have to go," Lisette repeated more emphatically. Part of it was that she couldn't afford to have Cecile and Aunt Josephine angry with her again, not two days in a row. And part of it was that, deep inside, she was very, very frightened. "I'll be back tomorrow," she mumbled, not sure yet if she meant it.

She didn't look at Gerard as she started down. And when she did look back — about halfway down — he was looking down the hill after her, but not quite in the right direction.

9.

If she'd been home, Lisette would have talked about the ghost to her father, or even to her mother. But Aunt Josephine didn't seem the kind of person who would take this sort of news well.

So Lisette didn't say anything about Gerard during lunch, or during the diaper-changing/diaper-washing session that followed. ("Lisette should do it," Cecile suggested sweetly. "She's used to babies and probably feeling homesick." But Aunt Josephine insisted they take turns.) Still, Lisette thought, if the opportunity arose during the bicycle ride to or back from Sibourne, she planned to ask about ghosts, since Cecile had mentioned them. She just wasn't sure what the opportunity would look or sound like.

She rode Aunt Josephine's bicycle, since Cecile's was too small for her and Uncle Raymond's too tall. That left Aunt Josephine riding Uncle Raymond's bicycle, which meant she had to wear a pair of Uncle Raymond's trousers, and she'd obviously hoped Lisette would be the one to do that.

"What we have to do," Aunt Josephine said as they rode side by side down the road that led to the town, "is buy a little bit here and a little bit there. I got two extra ration books through the black market, an adult's and a child's. But as far as anybody knows, there's only the three of us, so we can't use more than one adult and two children's coupons in any one place."

Lisette nodded. She wasn't used to all these hills and she was saving her breath.

"The hardest thing has been getting enough milk. Rachel, of course — she's just beginning to have solid foods. But the other small ones, too, they really should have milk every day. I don't get milk with the adult books, so I've been giving Rachel what she needs and watering down what's left for the others. Are you willing to give up your allotment?"

"Fine," Lisette said, although she thought it wasn't fair: she was a child, too.

And two extra ration books for four extra children, not including Rachel. So much for her parents' idea that she'd eat better here than in Paris.

But Aunt Josephine must have guessed what she was thinking. "Don't worry. We have the vegetable garden, and I've done well trading my cigarette coupons for grapes and peaches. There's always somebody who knows somebody." She must have guessed that Lisette still needed cheering, for she added, "Want to share a secret?"

Lisette nodded.

"You may have noticed that Cecile likes to keep everything. She doesn't know it, but I sold one of her outgrown dresses for yesterday's chicken." She put her finger to her lips to indicate not to tell and almost fell off the bicycle.

Lisette knew it was mean of her to let this news lift her spirits, but somehow it did.

Aunt Josephine and Lisette went to several stores to get their little bits of milk and flour and the one egg each that they were allotted for September, except that they only got two because it was so late in the day and most merchants had sold out already. Still, it *was* better than in Paris, where there were long lines for everything, and if you didn't get there early, you might as well not even wait because there'd be nothing left.

However, Aunt Josephine was self-conscious and grumpy about having to wear Uncle Raymond's trousers. Sure that everybody was staring at her, she felt she had to explain to clerks and other customers in every store how she normally wouldn't dream of wearing pants but that she was using her husband's bicycle and it was impossible to ride a man's bicycle and look modest at the same time with a skirt.

Lisette didn't think anybody cared, and for a while it seemed as though Aunt Josephine's embarrassing embarrassment would be the worst part of the trip. But as they were getting ready to start back, making sure that their baskets were secure on their bicycles, two German soldiers stepped out of the restaurant directly across the street from them.

One said something to the other in German. They both laughed, then the second man answered, then they laughed again.

Even Lisette thought they were looking at Aunt Josephine.

Aunt Josephine's face turned bright red. Lisette couldn't tell if she was more angry or mortified. In any case, her hands were shaking, and she suddenly became clumsy, unable to manage the bindings. Just as the Germans crossed the street, still talking and laughing, the package containing the noodles slipped out and dropped to the ground.

Lisette, Aunt Josephine, and one of the Germans all leaned down to get the parcel. Lisette picked it up first, and Aunt Josephine snatched it away.

The German who'd tried to help — a lieutenant, by his uniform — straightened and smiled. "Hello, *Fräulein*," he said.

"I'm not a *Fräulein*," Aunt Josephine said, readjusting the packages, refusing to look at him. "I'm not even a *mademoiselle*. I'm a *madame*."

"And a very pretty young *madame*," the German said. "My friend and I, we thought you were sisters."

For the first time, Lisette looked up. Her father was the oldest of the Beaucaire children, and Aunt Josephine was the youngest, with almost twenty years in between, but Lisette had never thought of her aunt as being young. Now, however, seeing the appraising expression on the German lieutenant's face, Lisette glanced at Aunt Josephine and reevaluated everything. She *did* look younger than her thirty years; and, with her light brown hair ruffled by the breeze and her blue eyes made brighter by her blush, she *was* pretty. Lisette could see why the German would look at Aunt Josephine the way he was.

Feeling unsettled, Lisette glanced away to the second German soldier, who wore a captain's insignia. But that made things worse, for he had much the same expression as his companion and he was looking at *her*. Lisette pretended she hadn't noticed. She looked at her feet, hunched her shoulders, and folded her arms in front of her.

Aunt Josephine had seen what was going on. "I'm much older than I look," she told them. "And she's much younger."

The lieutenant said something to the captain in German, possibly translating. Whatever it was, they both found it amusing. Then, to Aunt Josephine he said, "Here, let me help you." Short of hitting his hands away, there was nothing Aunt Josephine could do. He tied the packages to the basket so that they couldn't bounce out.

"Mine's fine," Lisette said as he turned to hers.

He checked anyway. "Quite a bit here," he told them. "You must have a big family, *madame*."

Was he suspicious, or just trying to make conversation? He was still smiling. But Lisette thought her aunt wore a guilty expression, and *she* probably did, too.

"Much of this is ice to keep the milk cold," Aunt Josephine said. "And our neighbors are elderly, so I do their shopping, too."

"Ah," the man said. "Kindhearted as well as beautiful."

"Thank you for your help," Aunt Josephine said. "Come, Lisette."

What a good spy she'd make, Lisette thought. *She's gone and given my name away.* But she didn't say, "Yes, Aunt Josephine." She just got on the bicycle and started pedaling.

The lieutenant called after them, "Perhaps we'll meet again, *madame, mademoiselle*."

The captain blew a kiss. Lisette wasn't looking, but she could hear it.

As they reached the outskirts of the town, with no sign of the Germans following, Aunt Josephine regained her composure. "That was a rather exciting marketing trip, wasn't it?" she asked, sounding lighthearted and — in the end — flattered by the attention.

On the whole, yes, Lisette thought. Except that the memory of the way that man had looked at her made her shiver despite the warmth of the sun on her arms.

10.

Monday, September 2, 1940

Back at the farmhouse, Lisette and Cecile took the clothes down from the laundry line. While Aunt Josephine started to prepare dinner, the girls did the ironing. Lisette knew how to iron, though at home in Paris her mother had one of the new electric irons, and Aunt Josephine only had the kind you heated on the stove. Cecile was only good at flat things: dinner napkins and handkerchiefs and some of the skirts, which left Lisette with shirts, blouses, dresses, pleated skirts, and the boys' pants.

After dinner, Louis Jerome and Etienne did the dishes, then everybody gathered in the candlelit living room because once again the electricity had gone off at six o'clock. Aunt Josephine had unraveled one of Cecile's old sweaters to reknit it into winter outfits for baby Rachel. Anne was helping her, sitting with her hands held apart while Aunt Josephine wrapped the yarn around them. Emma and Cecile were playing cards, but they kept showing their hands and dropping their cards, so they were no fun to play with. Louis Jerome was playing with Rachel, making faces and shaking her rattle so that she squealed with laughter, and Etienne was reading a book about planes that looked much too old for him.

"May I get a book to read from the study?" Lisette asked.

Aunt Josephine nodded while Cecile looked up from her cards and said, "Those are grown-up books. I have some in my room —"

"No, I was in the mood for a grown-up one."

Cecile looked at her as if she were crazy, but she abandoned Emma anyway. "Will you read it to me?" she asked.

With a glance at Aunt Josephine, who didn't look as though she was paying attention — but with mothers you could never be sure — Lisette said, "Certainly."

"Be careful with the candles," Aunt Josephine warned.

Cecile opened the huge doors at the end of the hall on the first floor, behind the staircase. "There are some over here that have pretty pictures," she said.

Lisette followed her. Cecile was talking about a section that had books on photography. Because Uncle Raymond was such an organized person, the photography section was also where he had a shelf for his photographic equipment: cameras, special papers and trays, bottles of chemicals. Uncle Raymond — Lisette's father had used to complain after family gatherings — tended to make a nuisance of himself with his picture taking. Here, the one wall without bookshelves was covered with framed photographs of Cecile and Aunt Josephine, and there were other pictures on just about every flat surface in the room.

Lisette bypassed the photography section and continued examining the shelves until she found a copy of the *Encyclopedia Larousse.*

"That looks boring," Cecile told her.

Lisette brought the book to the desk. "What's this for?" she asked, indicating the red cloth draped over the desk lamp.

"It's something to do with Papa developing his pictures. He can't use light, except red light is all right. Look at this picture of when I was five. Wasn't I cute?"

"Mmm-hmm." Lisette was trying to find out what sorts of things were going on in the world during 1314. It was before the Protestant Reformation, but after the Crusades.

"What are you looking for?" Cecile asked.

"Just looking. Hold that candle still." It seemed that most of the Middle Ages were one big lump. The book talked at great length about serfs and the role of the Church, but there were few specific dates. Apparently Gerard had died in time to miss the Black Death.

"Are you through yet?" Cecile asked.

"Isn't there a list of who was king when?"

Cecile shrugged. "Who cares? Let's do something else. Let's go back with the others."

She'd never find out anything this way. Lisette closed the book and returned it to its place. In Paris, there were all sorts of wonderful museums staffed by knowledgeable people who no doubt had the information she needed at their fingertips. But Sibourne wasn't Paris. Lisette wondered if the town even had a library.

They walked back to the living room, where Lisette had no sooner sat down than Cecile suggested, "We could brush each other's hair."

"All right," Lisette said, though she suspected that she would be doing most of the brushing.

Cecile ran to get a hairbrush, then settled herself in front of Lisette. "How about if we tell each other stories while you brush?" she suggested.

"What kind of stories?"

"Ghost stories," Cecile said a bit too quickly.

Lisette brushed Cecile's hair, which was the same light color as her mother's, but finer and straighter. "I don't know any," she said.

"Then tell me, what's the spookiest thing you've ever seen?"

Lisette worked her way through a tangle. "Aunt Louise with her hair in curlers."

"Lisette," Aunt Josephine warned.

But Lisette had gotten Cecile giggling, and she started talking about a teacher in her school — her old school in Nice — who had hair that always stuck out in all directions. *This must be hard for her, too,* Lisette realized. Cecile was used to spending her summers here, but she had never been to the school in Sibourne either.

After Aunt Josephine finished wrapping her yarn, it was time to get Rachel, Anne, and Emma ready for bed. While Aunt Josephine was upstairs reading the twins a bedtime story, Etienne started telling his own ghost stories, which made little, if any, sense. Lisette finally said, "Your turn to brush, Cecile."

Etienne stopped talking midsentence and Louis Jerome, who'd been looking through his stamp collection, closed his book with a snap. They were both out of the room before Cecile and Lisette had exchanged places.

Now what was that about? Lisette wondered. She said, now that they were alone, "So, Cecile, if you were going to tell a ghost story, what kind of ghost would it be?"

The brush caught in a tangle, and Cecile dragged it through.

"Be careful!" Lisette snapped, holding her hands over the spot that still tingled. "Go slower."

"Sorry," Cecile said.

"Ouch!"

"Sorry."

"OUCH!"

"Sorry. If you brushed it once in a while, it wouldn't be so tangly."

"I *do* brush," Lisette protested. "But my hair's thicker and curlier than yours. You can't — ouch! — Here, that's enough."

"No, no, I've got it," Cecile said. "Just this one more tangle, then it'll be easier."

Lisette tried not to squirm.

Cecile said, "He'd be young."

"Ouch. Who?"

"The ghost."

It was hard to concentrate on the conversation. "How young?"

"My age."

"Ouch! Cecile! Give me the brush."

"No, wait. Let me put it up with a rubber band."

"I don't want it up with a rubber band. I can never get those things out without having to cut — *Ouch!*" Lisette lunged for the brush.

Cecile yanked it away in time. "Be that way." She was wearing her hurt, sulky expression. "I'll do Etienne's hair."

"Fine," Lisette called after her. She remembered how Etienne and Louis Jerome had practically fallen over each other trying to get out of there. "If you can find him!" She rubbed her scalp. Finding out what

Cecile knew about Gerard wasn't worth the pain.

Except, she thought, that she *had* learned something.

Cecile had described him as looking to be her own age.

And even Cecile should be able to tell the difference between ten and thirteen.

11.

Tuesday, September 3, 1940

The next morning dawned gray and rainy, and it looked as though it would stay gray and rainy all day. When Etienne came back in from feeding the rabbits — a twenty-second dash from the porch door to the rabbit hutch and back again — Aunt Josephine carried on for at least half an hour about the mud on his shoes. Lisette was relieved. There was no way Aunt Josephine would permit her to play outside, and there was no excuse Lisette could give for going up the hill. So it wasn't her fault that she wouldn't be able to keep her promise to Gerard.

At first, Aunt Josephine announced that it was too wet to go into town. There was enough milk for

Rachel, if the others did without, and since it was so cool in the basement, the ice hadn't melted from the day before, so the milk would keep all day. But after breakfast and the regular morning chores, the rain that had looked to keep on forever had lessened to a dismal drizzle. Rachel was in a wretched mood, crying with a bone-jarring twang that was worse than nails on a blackboard. It reminded Lisette of home. "Probably teething," Aunt Josephine said. She poured some whiskey on her finger and ran it over the baby's gums, but still Rachel fussed. Aunt Josephine decided to go marketing after all.

"Let's play hide and seek," Cecile suggested before Aunt Josephine had pedaled to the bottom of the drive.

"Your mother said we were supposed to clean our rooms," Lisette said.

"My mother isn't here," Cecile pointed out. "You're it."

The children scattered.

"Three quick games," Lisette called after them. "And then the cleaning." Why did she have the feeling nobody was listening? "Then, the sooner we finish, the sooner we can play some more." To herself she thought, *I'm beginning to sound like my own mother.* It was a scary thought.

But after three games, Cecile said, "I never get to be it, because I'm such a good hider. Please, please, please, let me be it!"

"Oh, all right," Lisette said, because she'd thought of a good spot. She ran upstairs and hid in Aunt Josephine's armoire, crouched in the corner behind a long evening dress.

After a while she heard Cecile enter the room. Anne was with her — apparently Cecile had found her first — and Lisette held her breath so that neither of them could hear her. Cecile opened the armoire but didn't look closely enough to find Lisette. "Bed?" Anne suggested, perhaps the first time Lisette had heard her say anything that wasn't a response to a direct question, and then they were gone. From the hallway, she heard Cecile call out shrilly, "I see Etienne behind the armchair." And then she found Emma under the bed in her room, where she'd hidden during each of the three previous games also. All four of them went running down the stairs, laughing and shouting. Lisette knew Louis Jerome was downstairs because he hadn't come up with her. She waited patiently for Cecile either to come back after finding him and conduct a more thorough search, or give up.

After a while her back got tired, and she very carefully shifted position. Later, her knees got sore, so she stretched her legs out. She'd be sure to hear Cecile coming back up the stairs, and she could conceal herself better then. After more time passed, she got so tired of being in the armoire, she realized she was wishing Cecile *would* find her. She shifted position yet again, not taking care to be quiet. She sighed.

Eventually Lisette opened the door of the armoire. No sign of Cecile, except that she had left the edge of the comforter up when she'd checked under the bed.

Lisette moved quietly into the hallway — nobody there — and down the stairs. Still nobody.

From the living room she could hear Rachel banging her rattle on the floor, which meant that someone had gotten her out of her bassinet.

Stealthily Lisette eased around the corner. Emma was on the floor playing with the baby. Anne and Louis Jerome were attempting to construct a house of playing cards on the coffee table. And Cecile was arranging Etienne's hair. So far, she had it up in five little rubber-banded tufts topped with barrettes. Etienne didn't appear to be having nearly as much fun as Cecile was.

Lisette cleared her throat.

Cecile looked up. "Oh, there you are."

"Why didn't anybody tell me the game was over?" Lisette demanded.

"The game isn't over," Cecile said. "We just all got bored looking for you. You're it again."

"I am *not* it," Lisette protested. "And you're supposed to be cleaning your rooms."

"Oh, sure," Cecile said. "Get us to do your work while you play."

"I am not —" Lisette started, but Etienne suddenly shouted, "Somebody's coming."

Lisette ran to the window, knowing that if he was

simply intent on getting away from Cecile, Etienne could have tried this long ago. Now she, too, could hear the clump of horse hooves on the driveway and the crunching of wheels on gravel. But it would take a few more seconds before the approaching vehicle made it around the curve in the driveway that would bring it into sight.

Etienne put on his gas mask, pulled it down over his face, and headed for the kitchen and the basement door. He was the only one of the children who reacted according to Aunt Josephine's plan. "It's every man for himself!" his muffled voice proclaimed.

A bicycle horn honked.

"It's Monsieur Maurice and Maman," Cecile said as the battered cart pulled into view. "Don't bother with the basement. Everybody in the kitchen."

"What if she invites him in for coffee?" Lisette asked as finally the children began to move.

"She always invites him in," Cecile said. "He always says no."

Maurice pulled up on the reins. Now Lisette and Cecile could see that Aunt Josephine's bicycle was in the back. Had she had some sort of accident? Maurice was lifting the bicycle out of the cart.

Cecile gave Lisette a worried look as Maurice approached the back door, which opened out onto the porch, which opened onto the kitchen. "Everybody in the basement," Cecile screamed, nearly shattering Lisette's eardrum.

"Noise," Lisette told her. "We need to make noise to cover up the children's noise."

The two of them headed for the porch.

"Maman, Maman," Cecile called, at the same time Lisette shouted over her voice, "Aunt Josephine, are you all right?"

"What happened?" Cecile asked.

"Is the bicycle broken?" Lisette asked.

"Hello, Monsieur Maurice," Cecile said. Then to her mother, "What's Monsieur Maurice doing here?"

"Is it still raining?" Lisette asked, having run out of good questions.

"Yes, yes," Aunt Josephine said. "Everything is fine. Just put the bicycle over there, Maurice. That's fine. Thank you. *Cecile! Lisette!* Please."

Cecile and Lisette fell quiet at Aunt Josephine's tone of reprimand. There were no telltale noises from the stairs or the basement.

"Let's have some coffee," Aunt Josephine said. "We're both soaked."

"Well," Maurice said, "if you're sure it won't be inconvenient."

Aunt Josephine seemed suddenly to realize the possibility that the children might be up out of the basement. "Sometimes the house *is* a bit messy with these two girls . . ." she said hesitantly.

Maurice looked ready to leave then, but Cecile said, "We've spent all morning cleaning." Lisette could tell Aunt Josephine took this as a message that the children were safely hidden. "Come in," she insisted to Maurice.

Lisette tugged Cecile aside. "She's going to see that we didn't clean," she hissed. "And then she'll be angry."

Cecile shook her head. "If she complains that we didn't do a good job, I'll tell her she's always criticizing. She always feels guilty when I cry and tell her nothing I do pleases her."

It wouldn't work with my *mother,* Lisette thought, *but Cecile should know.*

In the kitchen, Aunt Josephine spooned the last of a package of coffee into the pot. "This is the good kind," Aunt Josephine said. "Real coffee, not ground acorns or beans. Just what we need to take the chill off after being caught in a downpour."

But there was more to it than that, Lisette suspected. Aunt Josephine was shivering and Lisette doubted it was just the cold, because Maurice wasn't shaking.

"You look like you've seen a ghost," Cecile said.

Aunt Josephine whirled to face her. "Would you stop talking about ghosts?" she snapped shrilly.

There was a moment of strained silence; the hiss of the gas burner was the only sound.

Then Aunt Josephine said, "Cecile, get the cups out. I'm going to put on some dry clothes."

While Cecile acted as hostess, Lisette followed Aunt Josephine into the hall.

"I'm fine," Aunt Josephine told her. Then, lowering her voice, she said, "Have you been frightening Cecile with ghost stories?"

"No," Lisette said. "Truly. It's Cecile who keeps mentioning gh —"

"This business of a German ghoul with awful wounds and . . ." Aunt Josephine was for once at a loss for words.

"*Cecile* was trying to scare *me*," Lisette protested. "I never said anything about ghosts at all."

"The thing is," Aunt Josephine said, "I think . . . never mind." She turned to go up the stairs.

"There *is* a ghost," Lisette said so that her aunt wouldn't be afraid, "but —"

Aunt Josephine must have thought that Lisette was simply trying to finish the statement *she* had started. She turned back with a sigh. "I thought I saw something, once. I don't know what it was, but it wasn't a ghost. And whatever it was, it wasn't the way Cecile described it. It looked like a young man — well, my age when your uncle and I were just married and we first moved in here. Up on that little hill beyond the barn — I thought I saw . . ." Aunt Josephine shook her head. "I don't know what I saw. But that's how ghost stories get started. There's nothing up there to be frightened of, Lisette."

Aunt Josephine's age when she and Uncle Raymond first bought this house ten years ago. That would make the ghost about twenty. Either Gerard had a disconcerting number of companions or he himself had a disconcerting tendency to vary his age. Lisette stopped trying to figure it out when she realized Aunt Josephine was trying to set her mind at ease and was worried that she found the idea of a ghost frightening.

"I think it best that you try to put all this supernatural nonsense out of your mind." Aunt Josephine was saying, still not convinced that Lisette hadn't been telling Cecile stories.

And she never would be, Lisette realized. So she said, "I'll try."

"Good," Aunt Josephine said and once more started up the stairs.

"But if it wasn't the ghost that scared you," said Cecile, standing behind them in the hall that led from the kitchen, where neither of them had noticed her, "then what *did* frighten you?"

Aunt Josephine glanced at Lisette before answering Cecile, and in that glance, Lisette knew. "There was just this German officer who was making me nervous."

"Do you think he knows?" Cecile asked.

Aunt Josephine shook her head. "No."

Before she could say anything else, Cecile said, "We shouldn't have taken them in. They'll get us all killed."

"Cecile!" Aunt Josephine sounded genuinely shocked. "I don't think he suspects anything. I think he's just interested —" She stopped, as though Lisette and Cecile were too young to understand. But Lisette had seen the look that officer had given her, and she suspected she knew exactly what he was interested in.

Cecile didn't look convinced.

"You come upstairs," Aunt Josephine told Cecile. To Lisette she said, "You entertain Monsieur Maurice."

In the kitchen, Lisette saw that Cecile had set out cups, napkins, a bowl with a tiny bit of sugar and another with milk, and even a plate of biscuits, everything ready so that there was nothing for Lisette to do except sit there and wait, with nothing to say to Maurice.

After a while, Maurice said, "So, how do you like Sibourne?"

"Very much, thank you," Lisette lied.

"You must be looking forward to school — next week, isn't it?"

Obviously Maurice knew nothing about being thirteen. Lisette just smiled politely.

After another while, Maurice said, "That cousin of yours, she's a very lively girl."

"Yes," Lisette said.

"My wife and I, we've watched her grow up every summer since she was born."

Lisette continued to smile.

"Seen the ghost, have you?"

"Excuse me?" Lisette said.

"Your cousin, she mentioned the ghost. I thought he'd gone away, but apparently he's come back."

"Gone away?" Lisette asked. "Come back?"

"I've lived here all my life," Maurice said. "As you can imagine, that's quite a long time."

Lisette found her polite smile again.

"As a boy, I used to climb all over these hills. Got myself lost in the woods more than once. Came nearer to drowning than my mother ever suspected. But that hill by the new barn, between my property and your uncle's — this was when the land belonged to the Martinage family, before your family ever moved in . . ." Maurice nodded, having either lost track of his sentence or getting caught up in his memories of the former owners.

"What about the hill?" Lisette asked. Maurice was obviously the kind of person who was not particular and would talk to anybody on any subject.

"Haunted. By a ghost my own age."

"*Your* age?" Lisette asked.

Maurice chuckled. "My age back when I first was old enough to be on my own — five, six years old."

Personally, Lisette didn't think that five or six was old enough to be on your own in the country, but she didn't say so.

"We grew up together," Maurice said, "that ghost and me. Not that we ever talked, mind you. But I'd catch glimpses of him. Oh, sometimes I wouldn't go up that particular way for a year or two at a time. And sometimes I'd go up there and wouldn't see him. But when I did, it always turned out he'd kept apace of me. Ten, twelve years old. Fifteen, sixteen, seventeen, twenty."

"But then he went away?" Lisette asked.

"About the time I was in my mid-twenties, I didn't see him anymore." Maurice winked at her. "Probably because I finally reached the age of reason. Finally realized I was too old to believe in ghosts." He winked again.

Aunt Josephine came down then, wearing a dry dress, fussing about pouring the coffee. Cecile passed the plate of biscuits after taking two for herself.

Lisette nibbled on a biscuit and tried to keep a polite look on her face as though she were listening while Aunt Josephine and Maurice talked about neighbors and weather and food prices. Mid-twenties, Maurice had said. Maurice thought the ghost had disappeared because Maurice had stopped believing in him.

Lisette wondered if Gerard had really disappeared because he'd reached the age at which he'd died.

12.

Tuesday, September 3, 1940

By the time Maurice left and the children were back upstairs, Lisette was determined to see Gerard after all, to learn if she was right. The rain had finally stopped, but the grass and trees were dripping. Mud glistened on the side of the hill, and Lisette knew better than to ask if she could go out to play. Still, the perfect opportunity presented itself after lunch, when Aunt Josephine announced that she had a headache and was going to take a nap.

Before Aunt Josephine had made it to the top of the stairs, Cecile sidled up to Lisette. "I know what you're planning," she whispered. "And you better not, or I'll tell."

Lisette forced an I-couldn't-begin-to-imagine-what-you're-talking-about smile. "I was just going to suggest a nice game of hide and seek. I'll be it."

"Oh no you don't," Cecile said. "Hide and seek gets played *in*side."

"Well, I'm going *out*side for a few minutes," Lisette hissed. There was no telling how long Aunt Josephine's nap would last. Lisette fought the impulse to push Cecile out of the way.

Cecile took a step toward the stairs, and Lisette clamped her hand over Cecile's mouth. Just then Emma came around the corner from the living room.

"What are you doing?" Emma asked as Cecile tried to bite and Lisette tried not to yell.

"Go away," Lisette told her. Then, to Cecile she offered, "I'll brush your hair."

Cecile kept struggling.

Lisette took a deep breath and said, "I'll let you brush my hair."

Emma shook her head. "Don't let her brush your hair," she warned with a shiver.

But Cecile had stopped struggling.

"All right?" Lisette asked. "You let me go out for a little while and you don't tell your mother, then we'll brush each other's hair?"

Cecile nodded and Lisette removed her hand from her mouth. Cecile said, "Except that we'll brush first, and *then* you'll go out."

"No," Lisette said. "If your mother decides to get

up after only fifteen minutes or so, we can still brush while she's up, but I can't go out. That's the whole point. And I'll brush for as long as I was out. You can time me."

"I'll time you," Emma volunteered, as though she could tell time.

"Go away," Cecile told her. Then, to Lisette she said, "Brush first."

"Why do we always have to do everything your way?" Lisette asked.

"Because this is my house."

"Yes," Lisette said, "but whenever you stay at my house, you say we have to do what you want because you're my guest."

"You're not my guest," Cecile said. "You're a refugee."

"You little beast." Lisette grabbed for Cecile's hair.

"Fight! Fight!" Emma cried.

"Shhh!" Both Lisette and Cecile hovered over the little girl.

"Lisette!" Aunt Josephine called down from her room. "Get the children to play more quietly."

"Yes, Aunt Josephine," Lisette said at the same time Cecile said, "Yes, Maman." To Emma — and to Louis Jerome and Anne who had come running in from the living room — Lisette said, "We're not going to fight." She glowered at Cecile. "Five minutes," she said.

"You said for as long as —"

"That's only if I go out first."

"Brush first, and however long you brush, if you're gone longer than that, I'm going straight upstairs and telling."

"Fine," Lisette said. "Beast."

Ten minutes of brushing was all Lisette dared — five minutes of her brushing Cecile's hair, and five long minutes of Cecile brushing hers. Louis Jerome timed.

"Where are you going?" Etienne asked as she put on her boots afterwards.

"To check on the rabbits," Lisette told him.

"I fed them already this morning."

"I'm not feeding them, I'm checking them."

Emma asked, "Are you going to eat one?"

Lisette sighed. "No, I'm not going to eat one. I'm checking them."

"Checking for what?" Louis Jerome asked. "Is there something wrong with them? If they get sick —"

"Louis Jerome," Lisette said, "the rabbits are fine, I'm fine, everything is fine. Please keep the children from disturbing Aunt Josephine, all right?"

She could tell that he was certain she was keeping dire news from him, but he nodded.

"You're wasting time," Cecile said as Lisette tied on a kerchief to cover the dozen or so barrettes Cecile had fastened in her hair. Cecile was leaning on the doorway, making a show of looking at the clock.

"You can't start timing until I leave, or I'll count the time you took to get the brush."

"Hmph!" Cecile said.

Lisette had to assume that signified agreement. She closed the kitchen door behind her quietly so as not to rouse Aunt Josephine. As she closed the porch door, a gray and white paw reached out through the wooden steps, just barely missing her leg with out-stretched claws.

"See if you get fed today," Lisette told the cat, then dashed across the lawn and up the hill.

"Gerard! Gerard!" she cried. It had started raining once again. Did ghosts come out in the rain? It seemed a ridiculous question, but what did she know of ghosts?

"Lisette," Gerard said as clearly as though there had never been a problem with hearing him. He stepped out from among the trees and put his hands out as though to take hers; but then he remembered in time. Looking at her quizzically, he said, "Thou art wet."

"It *is* raining," she pointed out.

But perhaps it wasn't as obvious as she had thought, for he looked around, then said, "Oh."

In the gloomy light he wasn't nearly as transparent as he'd seemed that first day. But she could see well enough to tell that the rain went right through him. Then again, that was normal. As normal as things were around him.

"Gerard," she said, "I have to talk to you, and I only have a few minutes." Were minutes too advanced a concept for someone from the fourteenth century?

His expression was tense and wary, but that may have been due to the way she was acting, which she knew was less than calm and reasonable. Where should she begin? Did he know that he was a ghost? Should she tell him, or would that somehow change things irrevocably — cause him to disappear or, worse yet, start haunting in earnest? She couldn't believe that. She remembered his tendency to make the sign of the cross when startled or worried, and how Aunt Josephine had described him as looking sweet and lost, and how he'd been around Maurice for nearly a quarter century without ever doing anything to make Maurice frightened of him. He'd tried to keep her from falling down the hill — or rather, as he'd seen it, to keep the hill from swallowing her up. That wasn't someone to be afraid of.

"Yes?" he prompted, waiting for her questions.

"How . . ." she asked, "do you see me? I mean —"

"Thou — you are a ghost," he told her.

Well, at least she knew the word didn't have any magical effects.

He looked away, hugging himself as if for warmth. "At least," his voice had dropped to almost a whisper, "that is what I thought at first." His brown eyes met hers again. "But you aren't, art thou? *You*," he corrected himself impatiently.

She shook her head.

"I have seen ghosts before," he told her, "and at the start you were just as they were. But the more often I see thee, the more substance you have. And now . . ."

"Yes?" she asked, halfway between whisper and exhalation.

"My world is fading. And it is not only you that I can see, but . . ." he paused and gestured helplessly. "Ghost trees? Ghost squirrels?" He asked it as though she knew more than he did. "And though I know it is not raining, I can see the rain, not just because thy face and clothing are wet, but . . . as a shadow. Is there such a thing as ghost rain? The fading is worst when you are here with me, but even when you are not . . ."

"You're aware of the passing of time?" Lisette asked. Somehow, she'd thought of him as existing only when she was looking at him. With a start, she realized he'd just told her that he'd thought the same about her.

"Yes," he said slowly. "But sometimes time seems to be standing still, and other times it bounds forth in great leaps, as a deer that breaks cover and flees."

"A day," she told him, "between each of my visits."

He was surprised, she could tell, even if he didn't say anything. Instead he asked, "Do th— Do *you* feel . . . the same sort of fading?"

Lisette shook her head.

"Well," Gerard said softly. "And do you remember dying?"

Lisette's breath caught in her throat.

Apparently that was answer enough. "Well," he said again, once more averting his gaze. He started to make the sign of the cross but stopped halfway through. After a moment's hesitation, he completed the gesture. "I knew," he whispered. "Deep down in my heart I knew. I tried to convince myself it was just a dream. But it was too vivid. *This* —" he made a broad gesture that Lisette took to include everything, his current existence rather than just her, "this is more dreamlike. Time passing so strangely. No other people, just the ghosts."

"Gerard, I'm so sorry."

"Even being here," he said. "This is where I grew up. But I could not remember coming back. There is a gap, but I cannot tell where it began."

"Gerard."

He must have been able to tell from her voice that there was something wrong, for he got that wary look again, as though he knew there was more bad news coming.

"Gerard, you're not entirely grown up."

He looked at his hands, turning them palms then backs upwards. Lisette couldn't tell if he learned anything from them. Then he touched the lower part of his face. *Beard,* she thought. He was feeling for beard, or at least stubble. She knew her father's skin, even right after he shaved, didn't feel as smooth as a thirteen-year-old boy's would. Gerard touched his hair, which was longer than a boy from 1940 would wear it, though Lisette didn't know what it indicated to Gerard. Last, he moved his hand from the top of his head out toward her, comparing their heights. "How old am I?" he asked, sounding very exasperated.

"Thirteen."

He winced and bit off a groan.

"But you have been other ages," she told him. "My cousin, Cecile, who's ten, she thinks you're ten. And when my aunt saw you, she thought you were her age, which was twenty."

"Thy twenty-year-old aunt has a ten-year-old daughter?"

"That was ten years ago. And our neighbor, Maurice, who's — I don't know, seventy or eighty — he saw you when he was a boy, and you always looked whatever age he was."

"I am as old as whoever looks at me?"

He was beginning to sound sarcastic and annoyed.

"It's not my doing," she snapped.

He made the same gesture — hand to heart then extended to her — that he'd used when she couldn't hear him, apparently an apology.

"I'm sorry," she told him. It couldn't be easy, learning all in one day that you were dead and that you had to grow up all over again.

"This neighbor," Gerard said, "saw me when he was a boy?"

She nodded.

"But not after he passed his twenty-seventh year?"

Maurice hadn't been that specific, but, "No," she whispered.

"I don't understand: I continually reach twenty-seven then die all over again?"

"I don't know," she started, but then she said, "No. Aunt Josephine saw you ten years ago and you were twenty. You wouldn't have had time . . ." She didn't want to finish that thought out loud. "Gerard, can you leave this hill? Can you come down to the house?"

"What would happen if different people of different ages all saw me at once?"

That was something she hadn't thought of. "I don't know. Maybe you should avoid people. It's just that I have to go back or Cecile will tell my aunt where I've been, and she'll tell me I can't come back — I know she will. Can you see the house now?"

"I can see a vague outline. I can tell where it is."

"Come back with me." She extended her hand, but his touch was still just an icy breath of air.

He followed her, though when they reached the edge of the hill he still walked on earth that had eroded away centuries since. But the farther down they walked, the fainter he became, and she guessed from the way he looked at her that she was fading away for him, too.

"I'll be back tomorrow," she said.

And with the next step, he was gone.

13.

The next day Aunt Josephine announced that she would take Cecile marketing with her. Cecile, who saw it as a morning without chores, was pleased. Lisette, who saw it as a morning without Cecile, was also pleased.

Until Cecile came downstairs wearing Lisette's white sweater.

"That's mine," Lisette protested. She added, "You didn't even ask," though she knew she would have said no in any case.

"Cecile," Aunt Josephine said. But she was putting on lipstick and didn't seem honestly concerned. Aunt Josephine could apply lipstick without using a mirror, which Lisette thought was about as sophisticated as someone could get.

"It doesn't fit you anymore," Cecile said. "The sleeves are too short for your arms."

"It's mine. And it's the only one I have," Lisette said.

"Put it back, Cecile." Now Aunt Josephine took out a mirror to adjust her hat. "You have plenty of your own."

Cecile leaned in close to Lisette. "By Christmas you won't even be able to button it, and then Maman will *make* you give it to me. By spring *nothing* will fit anymore, and I'll be wearing all your clothes, and you'll have to wear Papa's old suits."

"Cecile, don't tease your cousin," Aunt Josephine said. "Put on one of your own sweaters and get moving. I'm waiting."

Lisette watched Cecile flounce up the stairs. Teasing was telling someone you'd forgotten to get her a birthday present when she knew very well that you *hadn't* forgotten. Teasing was holding up rabbit ears behind someone's head while the photographer was preparing to take the class picture. Lisette knew that in all likelihood she'd never have to wear Uncle Raymond's suits, but Cecile was right about one thing: Lisette was outgrowing her clothes. Her mother had already let down the hems of her dresses as far as they'd go. There was hardly anything to be had in the stores. And, as the oldest of the girl cousins, she wouldn't be getting hand-me-downs from any of her relatives. If the war went on much longer, she'd have to make due with the charity clothes gathered and distributed by the churches.

After Cecile and Aunt Josephine finally left, Lisette put Louis Jerome in charge of his sister, who was in one of her crying moods again, then she made the beds while Etienne rinsed the diapers, and the twins cleaned up the breakfast dishes. By the time she came back downstairs, Etienne had flooded the bathroom. She mopped up the water, sending him to the kitchen to supervise the dishwashing, because from what she'd seen while passing through the kitchen, the girls' idea of clean dishes didn't match hers.

After boiling the diapers, she went out in the backyard to hang the laundry and saw the cat, sitting by the back door, meowing piteously. Spying Lisette watching, it rolled over onto its back, exposing its snowy white belly. Lisette had to laugh at the friendly invitation. Obviously they'd gotten off to a bad start when she'd tried to pet it while it was eating. The poor starving thing had been afraid she was going to take its food away.

She opened the door and crouched down by the cat, who was still offering its belly. Lisette put her hand out, and the cat closed all four sets of claws on it. Lisette cried out in pain and jumped to her feet. She would have kicked the little beast except that it quickly moved out of range and began cleaning itself.

"You just keep away from me," Lisette warned, going back in to wash off her scratched arm. The first set of wounds hadn't even healed yet.

She was out in the backyard again, hanging the diapers on the line, when she heard someone singing — loudly and not very well — and then there was the honking of Maurice's horn and the sound of wooden wheels on the driveway.

Louis Jerome had been walking from room to room with Rachel and was now on the porch. Thankfully Rachel had at least exhausted herself and was only whimpering fretfully. Louis Jerome ran through the kitchen door to gather up the other children as Maurice came around the last bit of the curving driveway. "Whoa!" he told the horse. Then, to Lisette, "Hello, little one."

Lisette had asked Aunt Josephine if he was Maurice something or something Maurice, but she had admitted that she wasn't sure, so Lisette just said, "Hello," and estimated they were even since he was probably calling her "little one" because he couldn't remember her name. She'd only hung two diapers, which could conceivably pass as dustcloths, and now she stood in front of the laundry basket that held all the other diapers. "Aunt Josephine isn't here," she said. "She's already left to do the marketing."

"Ah!" said Maurice. "Well, seeing her is only part of why I came." He jumped down from the seat with more energy than Lisette would have expected from

such an old person and walked to the back of the cart.

Lisette heard a sound which for one dreadful moment she thought was Rachel crying, but then Maurice reached into the back and lifted out a goat. He set the animal on its feet and it again gave that wobbly cry.

"Didn't like that ride at all, did you?" Maurice said to the goat. To Lisette he said, "This one's a real homebody. Fuss over her a bit and she'll be your friend for life and never wander. You'll get . . . oh, maybe fifteen glasses of milk a day from her. Ever milked a goat?"

"No," Lisette admitted warily.

"Give me your hand."

Lisette winced. "You want me to touch her udders?"

"Ud*der*," Maurice corrected. "One udder, four teats, city girl. Of course you have to touch it. You don't get milk just by asking."

The goat's udder was warm and didn't feel as Lisette would have guessed, if she'd ever thought about it, which she hadn't.

"Up here, don't squeeze, just slip down. Up here, slip down." Warm milk squirted out and hit Lisette's foot. "Build a rhythm. Don't be rough, but you do need to have a strong grip."

"So I see." Lisette's hand was beginning to cramp already.

"All you need to do is convince the goat you know

what you're doing, and she'll let you do it. Milk her first thing in the morning and last thing at night."

"What's her name?"

Maurice laughed at her. "She's a farm animal, not a pet." But then he relented. "Name her what you want."

Lisette nodded. "And what do we feed her?"

"She'll browse and find enough to eat on her own. If she gets into that field of flowers back there, she'll think she's died and gone to heaven."

"She wouldn't, by chance, eat cats, would she?"

Maurice gave her a startled look.

"Well," said Lisette, trying to sound grateful since Maurice *had* done the family a very big favor, "thank you very much."

"Not at all." Maurice climbed back up onto the cart. "I thought your aunt might want some company going into town today. She was upset about something yesterday."

Lisette wanted Maurice to leave before he became suspicious about the diapers, but she was also curious. "Then you didn't see what happened?"

Maurice shook his head. "No, I picked her up on the road back. But the fact that she was bicycling in the downpour rather than waiting indoors in town for the weather to let up . . ." Maurice shrugged. "Something to do with the Germans, I gather."

Lisette gave a noncommittal grunt.

"Me," Maurice said, "I don't get involved in politics. At least the Germans are polite. When a person gets to be my age, politeness counts for something."

"I suppose," Lisette said.

"Well," — Maurice picked up the horse's reins — "tell your aunt that if she's afraid to go to town alone tomorrow, she can go with me." He started to ease the horse and cart around in a circle to get back to the road.

"She went with Cecile today." Lisette only said it so that Maurice would see that Aunt Josephine was bothered by the attention but not truly worried.

But Maurice cast a quick glance at the porch.

Which meant he'd seen something as he pulled up, and he'd assumed it had been Cecile. Lisette bit her lip in frustration. *Stupid*, she chided herself. *Stupid, stupid.*

But Maurice only nodded at her one last time and shook the horse's reins so that it started back down the drive.

When she was sure he was gone, she went back in the house, leaving the laundry where it was.

No sign of anybody.

"Children!" she called.

No answer.

With a sigh she checked the basement door. The flashlight was gone from its compartment, which meant the children were in their secret room and wouldn't come out until she went down there and fetched them. She tried banging on the floor and yelling, "Long live France," but there was no answer. So she got the second flashlight and went downstairs. "Long live France," she repeated.

Cautiously the door opened and Louis Jerome peeked out. "Is he gone?"

"No, he's right here behind me, watching every move you make."

Apparently little children didn't understand sarcasm. Etienne kicked the door shut.

"I was joking," Lisette called.

Nothing.

She sighed. "Long live France," she said yet again.

The door opened a crack.

"What if he comes back?" Louis Jerome's voice asked.

"I think he already knows you're here." Lisette jammed her foot in the door before Etienne could slam it shut again. Anne was starting to whimper. "I think he's known for a long time. He'd have to be deaf, blind, and stupid not to have noticed. That's why he always honks the horn before coming anywhere near us, to warn you away so everybody can pretend he doesn't know. But he brought us a goat so we can have goat milk."

Anne stopped mid-whimper. "Goat?" she said, wriggling in front of Louis Jerome.

"Goat?" Emma echoed, close on her heels. "What's its name?"

"We're supposed to choose," Lisette said. "My

recommendation is that whatever you choose, you do it before Cecile comes back. Otherwise she's going to insist on naming it herself. Pick something, and we'll tell her that's its name and she can't go around changing people's names — or things' names. By the way, *it* is a *she*." Lisette might have been from the city, but she knew that much. "Why don't you come out and meet her?"

"What if Monsieur Maurice comes back?" Louis Jerome asked.

Lisette refrained from telling him to wait in the basement, just in case. She said, "He's gone to Sibourne to do his marketing."

The children followed Lisette out into the backyard, where they found the goat eating one of the diapers from the laundry basket. Lisette jerked the diaper away, which caused the goat to follow her closer to the house, where the children waited. "Don't be afraid, she won't bite." Lisette wasn't positive of that, but she assumed it was true because if goats were dangerous animals, people would keep them behind bars in zoos rather than on farms.

Anne reached out a hand. "Soft," she said, which it wasn't, really, not like, for instance, a cat.

"We could call her Mimi," Lisette suggested.

"That's a girl's name," Etienne said in disgust. "How about Spitfire or Hawker Hurricane?"

"Those are planes," Lisette protested.

Obviously Etienne knew. He pulled his gas mask

down over his face to look like an airplane pilot's mask, then he put his arms out and started making plane noises while divebombing Anne.

But Lisette wasn't going to let herself get drawn into this. "You choose. Anne, you get to make the final decision." If she could have had baby Rachel choose, she would.

"Where are you going?" Louis Jerome demanded.

"For a walk."

"But what if —"

"Everything will be fine. Etienne, keep the noise down and stay close to the house."

Etienne ignored her, which was normal.

14.

For the first time, Lisette saw Gerard right away, without having to call him. In fact, he was waiting for her, crouched by the edge of the hill. Thankfully, it was the edge that she could see. His elbow was resting on knee, his chin on his hand, the picture of bored anticipation.

He stood as she approached and extended his hand to help her. But then he remembered and instead stepped out of her way. "Hello, Lisette." He gave that wonderful smile. "I am happy," — she heard the slight break as he caught himself and shifted to the more modern pronoun — "*you* could come."

"And I'm happy to see you," she told him. "Have you been waiting long?"

"A day."

She raised her eyebrows, unsure if he was only acknowledging what she'd said previously, that she came once a day. But he continued, "This time I could feel the whole remainder of the day pass. And the night. And *half* the morning?"

"Just about," she agreed. "That isn't normal?"

He shook his head.

"I'm sorry I can't come more often," she told him.

"I understand. Thy aunt would not permit it."

"*Your,*" she corrected.

Now he raised his eyebrows at her.

"*Your* aunt would not permit it," she explained.

"My aunt," Gerard said, "has not expressed an opinion. It is *thy* aunt who will not permit it." He kept a serious expression just long enough for her to wonder if he'd honestly misunderstood, then he smiled.

Lisette fought to keep her face from showing that her heart was breaking at the unfairness of his being dead. She sat down on the ground, fussing more than was necessary to make sure her dress covered her knees. It wasn't fair. He looked perfectly healthy. She could no longer see the background through him, and realized this had nothing to do with the light. If he'd looked like this that first day, she wouldn't have even guessed he was a ghost. Well, maybe she might have guessed, she had to admit. But she wouldn't have *known.*

Gerard sat crosslegged, facing her. "Thy — your," he said.

She nodded.

"Thine?"

"Yours."

He didn't speak the word, but she could see him try it out. Then he nodded.

Then a thought occurred to him. "Does everyone in your world talk as you do?"

"Well, no," she admitted. He looked startled, and she finished, "Only the people who speak French."

Again the flash of teeth as he smiled, then he said something totally unintelligible.

"What?"

The smile faded and he repeated the same gibberish.

"What?"

"Can you not hear me?" he asked, raising his voice, looking as though he was about to panic, no doubt remembering those first two days.

"I can hear you," Lisette assured him. "I just couldn't understand what you said."

"I said, that is why we have Latin," — he was watching her as he translated and his voice got slower and fainter — "so everybody . . . can understand . . . everybody." He leaned back, looking at her quizzically. "You do not speak Latin?"

"No," she admitted.

"You seem educated."

"Well, thank you." She was insulted. After all, he was the one who couldn't read. "I'm only going to be starting to learn Latin this year. We just use Latin in the Mass now. You know, *Hoc est enim corpus meum.*"

He was obviously shocked that she would use the words of the consecration so lightly. He made the sign of the cross, but apparently that was somehow different.

"I didn't mean that disrespectfully," she told him. "I just meant that I can understand *Gloria in excelsis deo,* or *mea culpa,* or *Kyrie eleison* — no, wait, that's Greek, isn't it? — but —"

He was looking at her as though her hair had turned green.

"Maybe priests talk to each other in Latin when they don't want the rest of us to understand," she said.

Gerard ran his hand over his forehead as though he was beginning to get a headache. "Let us not talk of Latin anymore," he suggested.

"That's a fine idea," Lisette told him. "What shall we talk about?"

"You spoke of war," Gerard said.

She nodded.

"With Germans?"

Again she nodded.

"Who are Germans?"

"I could bring a book with a map," she said, trying to remember history and geography at the same time. "Umm, Prussians?"

He gave her another of those Lisette-has-green-hair looks.

"Not from Italy or Spain. Not the Ottoman Empire, I don't think. Do any of those names sound familiar?" Apparently not. "Uh, Berlin. Bremen. It's where Mozart came from, maybe, and Beethoven, I'm pretty sure. The Hapsburg princes, I think, with the big noses and the lips . . ." She started to indicate how big, but she could tell from his face that he'd never seen the portraits that were reproduced in her history book. "Uh, Rhineland. Hamburg —"

"Rhineland!" Gerard practically jumped on the word.

"Rhineland," Lisette repeated. "Yes. Wonderful." It suddenly came to her: "Holy Roman Empire. I think."

"Franks," Gerard said.

"Franks," Lisette agreed.

"The Franks were our allies," Gerard said, not arguing with her, just considering out loud. "The Teutonic knights."

Teutonic: There was another word she could have used.

"They were . . . fierce. Not very smart, generally speaking, but fierce. They wore white robes with black crosses."

Lisette shook her head to indicate none of this was familiar. "The English are our allies now," she said, "but they aren't very good allies. They bombed some of our ships just so the Germans wouldn't get them. Brigitte — she's my best friend — Brigitte's cousin's husband drowned. The Germans have posters in Paris that say, 'The English are always willing to fight until the last Frenchman is dead.' We're hoping the Americans will be better."

It was hard to tell how much of this Gerard understood. Enough, apparently, for he said, "There were times I know of, too, when our allies caused more harm than our enemies." Then he asked, "Does the war with the Germans have anything to do with Outremer?"

"Outremer?" she repeated.

"The Holy Land."

"No," she said. "You're talking about the Crusades, aren't you?" Did they call them Crusades back then? They must have, because he was nodding. "The last one was 13-something." She'd just looked up the date but couldn't remember. "Before —" She couldn't say that: Before you died. "Early. Early 1300s." He knew what she meant just the same. "Were you a knight?" she asked. He looked so natural as a boy, she kept forgetting that he had the memories of a twenty-seven-year-old man. A twenty-seven-year-old who'd been dead for six centuries. "Like Lancelot and Galahad and Percival?"

"Who?"

Lisette tried to think back further. "Roland and Oliver?"

At least he knew the names. "No," Gerard said. "Not really. I belonged to the Order of the Temple of

Solomon, who are monks as well as knights."

"Templars. I've heard of them." Lisette said, delighted finally to be able to say so. "We learned about them when we studied the Crusades: Knights Templars and Knights Hospitallers."

By his expression, Gerard didn't think too highly of her lumping together his order with that of the Knights Hospitallers. More bad allies, she guessed. But he only asked, "So they survived?"

"Who?"

"The Templars."

"Oh," Lisette said. "No." He went all pale, reminding her of when she'd told him the year was 1940. It seemed she was always breaking bad news to him. "It's not just the Templars. There aren't any knights anymore." That certainly wasn't what he wanted to hear, she could tell, so she added, "Well, maybe there are ceremonial kinds of knights to guard the king of Belgium or the queen of the Netherlands. I'm not sure. But not, you know, to ride horses into battle or anything like that. Not anymore. Although maybe there are still Templars at parades and grand openings and things like that." She wasn't helping. "I don't know. Maybe." Lisette bit her lip to keep herself from babbling any further. She definitely wasn't helping. Gerard was resting his head in his hands, looking once more as though his head ached.

"Who fights," he asked, his voice muffled by his hands, "if there are no knights?"

"Just regular soldiers," she told him.

"Regular soldiers?"

"They don't wear armor because they have guns now, and guns can shoot through armor. Except the kind of armor on tanks, but they can't have a tank for each soldier, and besides tanks can't go very fast and they get stuck in the mud, which is like horses, I guess, but that's why there are no cars anymore, because they're using all the gasoline for the tanks. And there are airplanes now, too, which they didn't have back in your time. They travel in the sky." *Shut up, Lisette!* she told herself.

Gerard suddenly swept to his feet. "I'm going now."

"Where?" It was definitely her fault. "I'm sorry, I know I haven't been saying this right —"

He yelled at her, "I don't know where I'm going. Wherever it is I exist when thou aren't there." More softly, he finished, "I am tired and I am cold and I am hungry, and I have heard enough."

"Wait," she called after him as he started running down the slope. Guiltily she remembered how he'd called after her that day he'd gained his voice, and how she, afraid, had not looked back.

Gerard didn't look back either. He made it almost to the bottom of the hill before disappearing, which was quite a bit farther than he'd made it the day before.

Lisette could understand that he was upset. She'd

been saying one thing after another to get him upset ever since they'd first met.

But how could a ghost possibly be tired or cold or hungry?

15.

Wednesday, September 4, 1940

As Lisette started down the hill back to the house, she saw that there was a bicycle leaning against the bushes by the front door. It wasn't Aunt Josephine's or Cecile's.

Oh no, she thought. *The children. Now what?*

She wished longingly for the days in Paris when her parents worried about her and she wasn't responsible for anyone. But while she wished, she swung by the chrysanthemum field and grabbed handfuls of blossoms: an excuse, if the visitor, whoever it was, had not already discovered the children and was still open to excuses.

As she circled round toward the front of the house,

she saw that it was a woman who had come to call. That was better than a German officer, whoever she might be and whatever her reason for being here. The woman was sitting on the front step, though that didn't prove that she hadn't looked in the house before settling there, for the door was not locked. There were five or six cigarette butts crushed out by the woman's feet, an indication that she'd been waiting for a while. Lisette wouldn't have thought she'd been away long enough for someone to smoke five or six cigarettes, but even as she watched, the woman was lighting a new one from the end of the one she was just finishing.

"Hello, *Madame*," Lisette said, trying to sound neither guilty nor suspicious, but the way any normal thirteen-year-old would who'd just been out collecting fresh flowers and came back to discover a stranger on her aunt's doorstep.

The woman drew heavily on her new cigarette and the end flared bright red. It smelled more like burning rope than regular tobacco and wasn't rolled tight and smooth, so it must have been homemade. Lisette's father smoked, but he'd already said that once real tobacco wasn't available he'd give it up rather than make do with corn silk. The woman was finally satisfied that her current cigarette wouldn't go out, so she crushed out the old one, all before saying, "Hello, my dear. Is your mother home?"

"My mother doesn't live here," Lisette said, determined not to volunteer any information about Aunt Josephine, whom, she suspected, this woman did not know, or she wouldn't have mistaken Lisette for her daughter. The woman's movements were so precise, despite the fact that she seemed bristling with nervous energy, that she was making Lisette nervous. That was probably why she was so skinny, Lisette thought: nervous energy. Or maybe she was hungry. Some of the northern provinces had even less food than Paris. Had this woman come south begging? She looked to be closer in age to Lisette's father, who was fifty, than to Aunt Josephine. Her hair, which was cropped short and was all in curls, was almost midway in turning from black to gray. What was Lisette supposed to do about an elderly beggar woman?

But the woman said, "You aren't Josephine Le-Page's daughter . . . umm, Christine?" which proved that she at least knew Aunt Josephine, even if she wasn't a close friend.

"I'm her niece."

The woman sucked deeply on her cigarette. "Well, I'll tell you what, my dear: one of us had better give in or we'll both be sitting out here until the next full moon. And frankly, my behind is getting cold and sore from this step. My name is Eugenie Dumont, and I'm a friend of your aunt's, though she was not expecting me today. Shall I call you Josephine's niece, or Mademoiselle LePage, or what?"

"My name is Lisette."

Madame Dumont left the cigarette in her mouth and extended her hand to shake Lisette's. "Now, Lisette, are you going to go in and bolt the door behind you, or are you going to invite me in?"

So she had tried the door and seen that it was unlocked, Lisette decided. Had she seen the children? Had the children seen her? Were they safely down in the basement where they belonged or were they lurking in corners, ready to be discovered if she let this woman in?

"My dear," Madame Dumont said in exasperation, "eventually you are going to have to make a decision about something."

Presumably Madame Dumont had knocked when she first came. If the children hadn't hidden then, it probably meant that they were making too much noise to have heard. And if they were making that much noise, then Madame Dumont had no doubt already heard them. Since she hadn't mentioned hearing noises from the supposedly empty house, maybe all was as it should be. Lisette went to open the door, saying: "I'm sorry. I'm from Paris and I'm not used to country manners." It was both to explain her hesitation and to warn the children that she was coming in with someone.

Madame Dumont snorted before crushing out her cigarette.

The house was totally still, the front room empty.

"Would you like to wait here, Madame Dumont?"

Lisette asked, raising her voice as much as she dared, a final warning that she wasn't alone. "Or would you like to come into the kitchen?"

"I'd like something warm to drink," Madame Dumont said, raising her voice to match Lisette's, "if you don't mind."

Lisette felt her cheeks grow pink. Either this woman knew exactly what was going on, or she thought Lisette was a total fool.

Passing the staircase, she glanced up. No sign of anybody there.

In the kitchen, all was as it should be. Lisette put the flowers she'd gathered on the table then set the kettle on the stove.

Madame Dumont sat down at the table and lit another cigarette.

"Let me fetch a vase for these flowers," Lisette said. She opened the basement door and was relieved to see that the flashlight was missing from its niche. *Thank you*, she mentally told God. At least the children were where they were safest. "No, wait," Lisette said out loud, "I think she keeps the vase under the sink."

She found a white vase that was a bit too small but she crammed the flowers in it. *Hopefully they don't have any bugs*, she thought as she set the vase on the counter.

"We don't have any coffee left," she told Madame Dumont. "My aunt has been using bouillon."

"That's fine." Madame Dumont was putting the

ashes from her cigarette into her left hand, which hurt just to think about.

As far as Lisette knew, Aunt Josephine didn't have any ashtrays, so she got out a bowl for her visitor to use. She was just passing the porch door when she heard a faint thump from there. *Oh, no,* she thought. Out loud she said, "Here you go, Madame Dumont." She put the bowl on the table, making as much noise about it as she could.

Had Madame Dumont heard? She gave no indication that she had.

From the porch came a noise as though someone was dragging something. What was the matter with them? Didn't those children have any sense at all? "So," Lisette said as brightly and as loudly as she could, "Madame Dumont. Would you like a cup or a mug?"

"A cup would do nicely."

Another thump.

Lisette slammed the cup down on the table.

Madame Dumont glanced from her to the porch to the cup and back to the porch.

From which came the definite sound of something moving.

Lisette leaned in close to demand Madame Dumont's attention. "Do you think you want a saucer, too?" she shouted at her.

"My dear," Madame Dumont said, "I think we should see what's rattling around on your aunt's porch."

"Porch?" Lisette asked.

Another thump, and the sound of glass breaking.

"Porch," Madame Dumont said.

"I'm sure everything's fine there," Lisette said. "You know how old houses creak."

Something big crashed — possibly a chair tipping over.

Madame Dumont abandoned her cigarette to walk to the door. She opened it and Lisette tried to see past her. "I know your aunt is not a country woman," Madame Dumont said, "but, my dear, I would expect that even in Nice they would know better than to keep goats in the porch."

"Oh, no!" Lisette said.

Maurice's goat had been single-mindedly trying to determine what a porch tasted like. It had nibbled on a chair pillow that was now bleeding fluff all over the chair and the floor. The blackout curtains had two corners chewed out of them, as though the goat had wanted to make sure that both sides tasted alike. An end table was lying on its side, a broken vase beneath it held headless stems. At the moment the stupid goat was working on eating a philodendron plant, formerly almost two meters tall and currently lying on its side, at least half its potting soil dumped out onto the floor and trampled in with the pillow stuffing.

"Oh, this is all my fault," Lisette said, thinking, *Those stupid children.* "Our neighbor just brought this goat over, and I was afraid it would run away while I was picking flowers, so I brought it in here." It sounded like a seven-year-old's reasoning to her, but she didn't think Madame Dumont thought very highly of her intelligence anyway. "It must have been hungrier than I realized."

The goat left the philodendron and tried to munch on the edge of Madame Dumont's jacket. "My dear," Madame Dumont said, pushing the goat away, "goats don't eat because they're hungry. They eat to annoy humans."

Just then there was a thud from inside the house.

What more could possibly happen? Lisette wondered, but a moment later she heard Aunt Josephine call out from the front door, "Lisette?"

"In the porch," Lisette said.

Aunt Josephine must have seen the bicycle outside, for she looked worried. But as soon as she saw Madame Dumont, she smiled. "Eugenie!"

"Josephine!"

The two women hugged.

"And Lisette," Aunt Josephine said, sounding concerned, Lisette thought, and trying to hide it. No doubt she was wondering about the children. Both her voice and her smile were strained. "And . . . a goat. How . . . interesting. Lisette?"

Cecile appeared in the doorway. "A goat!" she squealed. "Where did it come from?"

"Monsieur Maurice brought it for us to milk," Lisette explained.

"What does goat milk taste like?" Cecile asked.

Lisette, Aunt Josephine, and Madame Dumont all shrugged.

"Well, Lisette," Aunt Josephine said, talking slowly and enunciating carefully, "maybe you should put the goat in the barn until we decide what to do with him."

"Her," Lisette and Madame Dumont corrected. Madame Dumont winked at Lisette.

"In fact," Aunt Josephine said with strained brightness, "Cecile, sweetie, why don't you get that bucket that we normally use to bring home the ice and you and Lisette can try to milk the goat?"

She was trying to get rid of them. Cecile was too interested in the goat to notice, but Lisette was sure of it. Aunt Josephine wanted to talk to her friend alone. This was getting more and more interesting.

16.

Wednesday, September 4, 1940

At first Cecile was so eager to milk the goat that she could hardly stand still long enough for Lisette to show her the way Maurice had shown her.

"What's the goat's name?" Cecile asked.

"Umm, I can't remember. I told the others, but I've forgotten now."

Cecile looked at her as though she were the stupidest person she'd ever met, but at least she didn't accuse Lisette of lying.

To divert her attention, Lisette asked, "What's the stray cat's name?"

"Mimi," Cecile said. "I named her after your cat."

Lisette didn't even answer.

After about five minutes of milking, Cecile got tired, which was a good thing since Maurice had said the goat should be milked in the morning and in the evening.

"I'm going back in," Cecile announced. "This is boring."

"I think your mother wants to talk with her friend alone," Lisette said.

Cecile was heading for the barn door. "She wouldn't mind me being there."

"Cecile," Lisette said, "stay here."

"You're so bossy. No wonder your parents couldn't stand you and sent you away."

Lisette gritted her teeth. "Do you want to play out here for a while, Cecile?" She tried to think of some game that would involve tying and gagging Cecile.

Before she could come up with anything, Cecile said, "Let's play family."

"No," Lisette said. "We did that this morning before breakfast, and last night, and yesterday morning, and —"

"I'll be the mother."

"No, you're always the mother, and I'm always the —"

"And you'll be the father."

"I don't want to be the father," Lisette protested. It didn't do any good. It never did.

"And the goat can be the baby. I'll sit down, and you put the goat in my lap."

"The goat is not going to want to sit in your lap, and I don't want to be the father."

"Alphonse, dear," Cecile said to Lisette in her version of a sophisticated lady's voice, "kindly fetch our baby, Lulu. I don't know *what* has become of our servants. They *don't* answer the bell. We'll have to *dismiss* them all and hire new ones."

Lisette stood there tapping her foot while Cecile batted her eyelashes at her.

"Alphonse," Cecile commanded. "I'm waiting."

All right, Lisette thought. "I'm sorry, dear —" she started.

"Magdalene," Cecile told her.

"I'm sorry, Magdalene, but the army has drafted me. I'm off to fight in the war."

Cecile jumped up and stamped her foot. "Alphonse, you have not been drafted."

"I'm sorry," Lisette said, picking up the pail of milk, "but I must go. And if I'm lucky," — this wasn't worth it: if Aunt Josephine wanted Cecile out of the house, let Aunt Josephine tell Cecile to get out — "if I'm *very* lucky, I may not come back."

"What a hateful thing to say!" Cecile was so angry, she looked ready to spit. "You beast! I'm telling Maman."

"What?" Cecile's reaction was beyond reason.

She pushed past Lisette and ran into the house, howling all the way.

With a sigh, Lisette followed.

Aunt Josephine and Madame Dumont were in the kitchen, Aunt Josephine looking as though she'd just hastily risen from her chair. Cecile had her face buried in her mother's skirt and she was wailing, "Maman, Maman, Lisette said Papa is never coming back from the war."

"I didn't —"

"Lisette!" Aunt Josephine was obviously shocked. "How could you say such a thing?"

"But I —"

"There, there, sweetie, Papa is safe, Papa will be coming back. Lisette, I can't believe you'd say such a cruel thing." But obviously she *did* believe it.

"I never said —"

"Hush, darling. Lisette didn't mean it. Lisette, tell her you didn't mean it."

It was, after all, the simplest way. "I didn't mean it," Lisette said.

"There, there, all over now," Aunt Josephine assured Cecile. "As a matter of fact, Madame Dumont has just brought us some good news about Papa."

"He's coming home, he's coming home," Cecile chanted.

"Well, yes and no," Aunt Josephine said. "He's not coming home, but Madame Dumont has some friends who know exactly where he is."

"Near here?" Cecile asked Madame Dumont. Madame Dumont nodded.

"Papa's coming home! Papa's coming home!"

"Cecile," Aunt Josephine said sharply.

"What?" Cecile must have recognized by her mother's tone that whatever was coming next was not going to be entirely good news.

"*I* am going to visit Papa. You will have to stay here with Lisette —"

"Why can't I come?"

"I'm sorry, you cannot. Papa will be arriving at night and he will only be there for a very short while and —"

"Is he coming by parachute?" Cecile looked eagerly from her mother to Madame Dumont. "He *is*," she said; it was the same conclusion to which Lisette had come. "I want to see Papa jump out of a plane with a parachute. Has he come to blow up some bridges?"

"Cecile, it would be very dangerous for Papa if anybody found out."

"I can keep secrets," Cecile said.

"Madame Dumont and I will be leaving after lunch," Aunt Josephine said. "I know it's a nasty shock to hear that Papa's going to be visiting so close to home and that you can't see him."

"Is Madame Dumont staying for lunch?" Cecile asked, having made — Lisette thought — a miraculous recovery from her nasty shock. "I can do a cartwheel, Madame Dumont. Would you like to see?"

Aunt Josephine said, "Madame Dumont is staying for lunch, so perhaps you can show her your cartwheels later. Lisette, would you please set out four places?"

So Madame Dumont was friend enough to be given lunch, but not to be entrusted with the knowledge of the presence of the children. *Poor children,* Lisette thought, *stuck in the basement, not knowing what's going on, while we eat lunch.*

Lisette kept watching Aunt Josephine, expecting some sort of signal regarding the children. But Aunt Josephine merely started cooking some pasta and breaking up a lettuce for salad.

Cecile ran to her room, then back downstairs to show off her ballet shoes, and chattered about lessons she'd been taking back in Nice, and how the teacher had said she was the most talented girl in the class. "Would you like to see me dance?" she asked Madame Dumont.

"Perhaps later," Madame Dumont told her, but Cecile put her shoes on anyway and did toe stands and grande jetés all around the table.

When lunch was just about ready and still Aunt Josephine had given no indication that she remembered the other children, Lisette said, "I think I need a bigger bucket for milking the goat. I'll look in the basement."

Downstairs, she tapped quietly at the secret door, realizing she risked giving Louis Jerome a heart attack. "Long live France," she whispered, "but just open the door a crack."

The door opened just wide enough for somebody — Louis Jerome, guessing by his height — to peek out.

"A friend of my aunt came to visit," Lisette said. "Do you think she saw any of you?"

Etienne poked his nose out — or rather, the nose of his gas mask, which was covering his face.

Louis Jerome said, "We were outside, still trying to think of a name for the goat, when we heard the sound of a bicycle coming up the driveway. We knew it was too early for Madame LePage and Cecile, so we ran in the house and looked out the living room window. When I saw it wasn't them, we came down here. I don't think she saw us. Why, did she say something about us?"

"No, you're fine," Lisette assured them. "She's staying for lunch, so you can't come up yet."

Emma wriggled in front of Louis Jerome. "We put the goat in the porch so she wouldn't get lost. Did you find her?"

"Yes, we did."

Anne came up under Louis Jerome's arm. "Softy," she said.

"What?"

"We named the goat Softy," Emma explained.

"She's not that soft," Lisette pointed out.

From behind the others she could hear Etienne complain, "You're the one who let Anne choose."

Anne grinned at her.

"All right," Lisette said, "Softy it is. Now everybody keep still and I'll come get you as soon as this woman leaves."

"What if she stays for supper, too?" Louis Jerome asked. "What if she stays for the night? What if she *did* see us?"

"She didn't see you," Lisette said again. "And she's only staying for lunch." Now was not the time to tell them that Madame Dumont was taking Aunt Josephine with her.

"But what if she *does* stay longer?"

"If she does stay, which she won't, I'll bring some food down for you. Now close the door again."

She could tell he was thinking, *But what if you don't come back?* but he didn't ask it. He closed the door and Lisette went back upstairs.

Madame Dumont smiled at her. "Couldn't find your bucket, my dear?"

She'd forgotten all about it. "Umm, no. I'll have to take a better look after lunch."

After lunch, however, Cecile talked Madame Dumont into going upstairs to see all Cecile's pretty clothes, and Lisette took the opportunity to ask Aunt Josephine, "Is she with the Resistance?" Now that the French army had surrendered, those who still fought the Germans were called Resistance fighters.

Aunt Josephine was washing the dishes while Lisette dried. She scrubbed at the pot before saying, "Yes."

"Then why couldn't the children have lunch with

us?" It wasn't that she *liked* the children. They were an awful nuisance, but she thought how frightened and hungry they must be in the basement, so she said, "If she's against the Germans, too —"

"Things aren't that simple, Lisette. People can be against the Germans and still hate the Jews. Just as they can be pro-German while sympathizing with the Jews. Or maybe they don't care about the Jews one way or the other."

"I suppose," Lisette said.

"It's like General de Gaulle. Some people think he's a saint who'll rescue France; others think he's only interested in himself. History books will make it all easy, deciding for us depending on the outcome. Looking back always makes things less complicated: 'The Roman Empire fell because of these four factors . . .' 'Napoleon didn't have a chance after Waterloo.' 'Marshal Pétain was the hero of the battle of Verdun but the villain in the capture of Paris.' The thing to remember is the Romans didn't know they were falling any more than Napoleon knew he was done for."

"Josephine, what nonsense are you filling that child's head with?" Madame Dumont stood in the doorway giving her throaty laugh. She had stopped smoking long enough to eat lunch, but she had another cigarette now. She took in a deep breath of it and said, "You aren't trying to talk her into being a supporter of that doddering old fool Pétain, are you?"

134

"No." By her tone, Aunt Josephine not only didn't find the idea reasonable, she didn't find it funny. She shook the excess water from her hands then reached for the towel. "I'm only saying that at this very moment there is probably some perfectly nice German family saying to themselves, 'Everything would be wonderful now, we'd have enough food, and our Papa would be home if only it weren't for those horrid French.'"

"My dear," Madame Dumont said, "there aren't any perfectly nice German families. If they were nice, they wouldn't be Germans."

Aunt Josephine laughed. "Where's Cecile?"

"Trying on her entire wardrobe, one dress at a time. I don't believe she's noticed I'm gone yet."

"I'll be ready to leave in just a few minutes."

Aunt Josephine went upstairs, and Madame Dumont laughed again. "Your aunt never ceases to amaze me," she told Lisette. "You must get her to tell you how we met." She took another drag on her cigarette — she always inhaled deeply as though each puff was the last one she'd ever get — then added, "Not in front of your little cousin."

And who could resist that? "How *did* you meet?" Lisette asked.

Madame Dumont looked at her for several seconds before saying, "It was on the road from Tours, in June, right before the armistice was signed. The Germans were bombing the city, and when the people tried to flee, the planes flew very low and strafed them. Do you know 'strafe' — to shoot with a machine gun?"

Lisette nodded.

Madame Dumont took another deep breath of cigarette smoke. "Sometimes when they were close enough, you could see the pilot's blue eyes. I lived in Tours — notice I use past tense: there's not enough left for people to live there anymore; some continue to exist, but nobody *lives* there. Your aunt had been visiting . . . your grandmother?"

"Cecile's grandmother — Uncle Raymond's mother."

". . . who was sick. She died? Before the bombing?"

Again Lisette nodded. She expected Madame Dumont to offer condolences even though Lisette wasn't related to the woman — adults usually said such things — but she only took another deep drag.

"So she had an extra reason to want to get out of Tours before the Germans flattened it or cut us off: Cecile was still in Nice and Josephine was desperate to get to her. So there were all these people, a few in cars, some in horse-drawn carts, most walking. Some pushing grandparents or luggage in wheelbarrows. And Tours had been jammed with people to begin with, refugees in from the countryside. And the French army trying to get around us — some heading toward the fighting, some running the other way. And the Germans. Strafing." Madame Dumont pantomimed a gunner.

Lisette had known this before, but it was hard to imagine Aunt Josephine in the middle of it.

"As we got farther, people started dropping their luggage; grandparents wandered off and got left behind. People would kill to get a ride in a car, then the car would run out of gas, be left in the middle of the road. We'd walk around it. And there would be dead bodies. We'd walk around them. Your aunt . . . her I met one time when the planes were farther off, bombing. There was an abandoned farmhouse, which was probably the stupidest place to hide, a nice big target. Several of us were there, standing in doorways, where the ceilings would be less likely to fall in on us. My dear, we could feel the ground shaking. Plaster dust fell on us like snow. A Gypsy wagon was in the front yard, lying on its side — the horses dead, a Gypsy man and woman dead. But there were two Gypsy children left alive, girls, too young to know what danger they were in. We'd all passed them on our way into the house, but Josephine went back to get them. Tucked one under each arm."

Lisette gasped, realizing Madame Dumont was talking about Emma and Anne.

"You think that was a brave thing to do?" Madame Dumont asked.

Lisette nodded.

"Perhaps," Madame Dumont said. "But what would have happened to your little cousin if her mother had been killed? Would the neighbors who'd taken her in for a week still be watching her — her in Nice, and the rest of your family in Paris and Tours? And nobody would have known. I didn't know Josephine's name at that point. She'd be four months dead now, and your family still wouldn't know — not for sure."

"What happened next?" Lisette asked, uncomfortable with the direction the talk was taking.

"Some old woman was screaming, 'We're going to die, we're going to die.'" Madame Dumont's cigarette was just about gone. She started to get another one, but then they could hear Aunt Josephine coming down the stairs, followed by Cecile, sniveling and complaining. Madame Dumont crushed out the old cigarette. "We didn't, of course," she finished. "Not all of us. Ready, Josephine?"

Lisette saw that her aunt was carrying a little overnight bag. "How long are you going to be gone?" she asked as Aunt Josephine leaned to kiss her.

"The drop is supposed to be tonight," Aunt Josephine said. "But it might get delayed due to weather or . . ."

"German patrols," Madame Dumont finished for her.

Aunt Josephine had the same not-in-front-of-my-daughter expression that Lisette's parents used. For the first time in her life Lisette realized she missed that look. Aunt Josephine continued, "I should be back tomorrow afternoon. If not, no matter what happens, I'll only wait one day. So, tomorrow or Friday afternoon. Make do with the goat's milk. There's no need to go into town. Lisette, it's past time you wrote to your parents."

Certainly, Lisette thought. *I can tell them Cecile is miserable, Aunt Josephine is working me to death, I've gotten a ghost angry with me, and there are German soldiers lurking about ready to discover the Jewish children we're keeping. Thank you for sending me here.*

Cecile wiped vigorously at her eyes. "I still don't see why I can't come," she said.

"Well," Madame Dumont said, "but you can't."

And with that they were gone.

17.

As soon as Cecile got over her heartbreak at being left home — which lasted about as long as it took for Aunt Josephine to shut the door — she went completely wild.

"You know what Maman told me?" she asked Lisette in a voice already high and strained with excitement.

"What?" Lisette asked.

"She told me I was to listen to you. You know what?"

Lisette guessed it at the same moment Cecile said it: "Maman's not home."

Cecile pushed a kitchen chair out of the way and positioned herself for a cartwheel.

Perhaps it wasn't that she didn't care; perhaps she was misbehaving to hide her worry. But in either case Lisette decided that, all things considered, this was probably something she didn't want to see. She went to get the children from the basement.

It was a very long day.

And every time she looked at Anne and Emma, she thought of them in the tipped wagon. For the first time she began to miss her parents, really miss them, not just resent that they'd sent her away. She even took a moment to wonder about François — and she thought of him as François, not as "the baby." She wondered if he was well.

In the afternoon there was a thunderstorm, and it came as no surprise to Lisette that Anne was afraid of thunderstorms. She clutched Lisette's sweater and howled as the storm drew closer and closer, the thunder coming almost simultaneously with the lightning. Cecile, who Lisette suspected was not nearly as afraid as she pretended, squealed loudly at each flash, which frightened Anne even more. Lisette finally had Etienne pull shut the blackout drapes so that they couldn't see the lightning. But they could still hear the bone-rattling thunder and Anne knew that, seen or not, the lightning was out there. Eventually the thunder moved on, but the rain still pelted at the windows and the wind howled. Anne sobbed herself to sleep despite Louis Jerome, who stood by Lisette's elbow asking, "What if the house gets struck by lightning?"

By the time Lisette remembered, after supper,

that the goat still needed to be milked, she was exhausted.

And she realized she'd made a foolish mistake.

It was still raining, so she couldn't milk Softy in the yard by the last of the daylight. She'd have to go in the barn. Though tonight the electricity had stayed on, there was, of course, no electricity in the barn. And even if there had been, she wouldn't have been able to turn on a light because of the blackout regulations. How could she milk a goat she couldn't even see?

She walked down the back steps carefully, but it must have been too wet out for Mimi the cat, who had apparently found dryer lodgings elsewhere. *At least I'm lucky in something,* Lisette told herself.

At first she thought she'd have to bring the goat back into the house and hope it wouldn't make too big a mess. But once she opened the barn door, she realized that there was enough daylight left if she stayed by the door and worked fast.

She stepped into the barn, out of the rain, and put down the stool she'd brought and the bucket. Something stirred in the darkness of the far corner, but before she could call out, "Here, Softy," the goat came up from behind and gently butted her.

Germans! Lisette thought in panic.

"Lisette?"

Her heart pounded frantically before she recognized that it had been Gerard's soft voice.

Obviously she was spending too much time with Louis Jerome; his tendency to worry was catching.

"Gerard." She whispered, too, though the children couldn't have heard even if they'd been on the porch, which they weren't; they were in the front room getting their hair styled by Cecile. "What are you doing here?"

As he came closer, she saw he'd found a filthy old rag of a towel that he had wrapped around him like a shawl. His longish brown hair was all plastered down and he was wet enough that he actually dripped.

"Oh, Gerard," she said, "is it raining in your world, too?"

His eyes widened, but he quickly looked away, hugging himself for warmth. *"I'm cold,"* he'd said the last time they'd been together, and she'd wondered how a ghost could be cold. "My world has faded away totally," he told her. "I can see nothing of it anymore."

She stopped in the act of reaching out to touch him, afraid to destroy the illusion.

"And after we parted," he continued, "I was so tired, I lay down on the ground, and I fell asleep. Lisette, I don't remember that happening before. Not since . . ." He bit his lip and looked at her with huge, frightened eyes. "Am *I* beginning to fade?"

"No," she said. Then, more emphatically, "No!" She nodded toward the towel. "Is that yours?" she asked. "Did it come from your world?"

He looked worried, as though she might be angry that he'd taken it. "No. It was just . . ." He pointed to show where he'd gotten it. "I'm sorry, I —"

"Gerard. It's all right. I just wanted to know if you

could actually touch . . ." — she'd almost said "real things" — "things from my world. Let me get a blanket for you." But it was freezing out here. How much good would a blanket do for someone whose clothes were soaked? His teeth were already chattering. "Or . . . you could come into the house."

Gerard shook his head emphatically. "What if your aunt saw me?"

"She's not here." Lisette sighed. "There is Cecile, though, and the other children."

Gerard was shaking his head again. "No. It's bad enough being thirteen. I would not want to be ten again."

"And Cecile isn't even the youngest," Lisette admitted. Would he shoot back and forth in age between her thirteen years and Rachel's six months depending on who was looking at him? And again the even scarier question: What would happen if more than one person looked at him at once? "Perhaps it would be safer out here," she said. "But let me try to find a blanket for you, and a change of clothes." She remembered he'd said before he was hungry. "And some soup." It couldn't hurt to try.

He gave that distractingly sweet smile that lit up his whole face, and he touched his hand to his heart.

Cecile must still have been arranging people's hair, because as soon as Lisette entered the house, she heard Anne call from the living room, "Lisette's turn."

Two words in a row: it may well have been a

record. *And after I put her in charge of naming the goat,* Lisette thought. *Traitor.* "I still haven't milked Softy," she shouted as she ran up the stairs. "I'm just getting my coat."

Nobody came to watch her, which was a relief because she really went into Aunt Josephine and Uncle Raymond's room. She got a pair of thick work pants and a heavy brown sweater from the dresser. Hopefully Aunt Josephine didn't miss Uncle Raymond so much that she looked through his clothes to be reminded of him. There were no shoes that she could find, so she took two pairs of woolen socks. From the chest at the foot of the bed she got the extra winter blanket.

Downstairs, she cut a slab of bread and ladled some of the soup that was left over from supper into a bowl. It was supposed to be tomorrow's lunch, but she could add more pasta later. She'd set the pot on the porch to cool and it was already lukewarm, but since Gerard hadn't eaten in six hundred years, he probably wouldn't be fussy.

When she got back to the barn, she found that he had milked the goat for her. Apparently *he* hadn't needed lessons. Apparently knights didn't spend all their time pulling swords out of stones and rescuing maidens.

"This is wonderful," Gerard said, just from the sight and smell of the meal. Lisette turned her back so he could get out of his wet clothes and into the dry ones. She sat on the milking stool, facing the open door, and petted Softy. Despite what Maurice had said, Softy didn't seem to realize she was a farm animal; she kept butting at Lisette's hand whenever Lisette stopped petting.

Behind her, in between mouthfuls, Gerard was trying simultaneously to change and carry on a conversation. "Where has your aunt gone?" he asked.

"A friend came to tell her my uncle is nearby. He's with the army and she hasn't seen him or heard from him since the occupation. Until today, we didn't even know for sure if he was still alive."

"So meanwhile you watch her children. How many are there?"

"Actually, only Cecile. But Aunt Josephine has taken in five other children, too. Rachel is the youngest — she's six months old — and Louis Jerome is the oldest. He's eight, though sometimes he sounds about eighty. Then there are the twins, Emma and Anne, who are three years old. And Etienne. I think he's five."

"Do you have a rope?"

"*Rope?*" Lisette echoed. "There was a piece about this long" — she held her hands apart — "by that post over there."

She peeked as he went to get it. He'd managed to figure out how all the modern clothes went on, but the pants were much too big and the rope was to hold them up. She turned to face him as he settled back

146

down, wrapped in Aunt Josephine's blanket, and took another spoonful of soup. "These are fosterlings?" he asked.

She had to stop to relocate her place in the conversation. "The children? Do you mean orphans? No, they're Jewish. Except for Emma and Anne. They're Gypsies. Hitler — he's the leader of the Germans — he thinks everybody should have blond hair and blue eyes."

Gerard paused to consider. The light had gotten so dim, she couldn't make out his face, only the outline of his form. "Why?" he asked.

"*Why?*" Lisette repeated. "He's crazy, he doesn't need a reason. He calls Germans the 'master race.' Everybody else is inferior, and Jews and Gypsies are the most inferior of all."

Gerard shook his head to indicate he didn't understand. "What are Gypsies?"

"I don't really know much about them," Lisette admitted. "They're a group of people who live out of wagons and wander from country to country . . ."

"Pilgrims?"

"No. They don't have any permanent homes; they always keep moving."

"Nomads."

"Yes," Lisette said. "Sort of."

Gerard wiped up the last of the soup with the last of the bread then put the bowl down on the floor. "Thank you," he said. "That was very good." As she opened her mouth to say you're welcome, he said, "So your aunt has taken in these children so that the Germans won't kill them?"

"Well, they wouldn't kill them," Lisette said. "They put them in work camps."

"I don't understand."

"They put them to work," she explained. "Factories. Farms."

"They put six-month-old babies to work?"

Lisette hated it when he got sarcastic. "Obviously not the babies," she said. "But the adults."

"Lisette," Gerard said, "that makes no sense. Who feeds all these children while the adults work? Who cares for them?"

Lisette rubbed her arms, wishing she'd worn a coat after all. She thought of the family in the train, the mother and the father, the grandfather and the two children. "I don't know. Maybe the ones who are too old to work."

Gerard sighed. He spoke slowly, hesitantly. "I know much has changed, but, Lisette, I have seen enough of war . . . and the governing of people . . ." — she almost thought he wasn't going to finish the thought — "to know that the weak and helpless are always the first victims."

She stood, so quickly that she knocked over the stool. "You think they're killing the children?" she said. "That's . . . crazy." But then she remembered she had just told Gerard that Hitler *was* crazy. *Still . . . Still . . .* she thought.

Yet Gerard would not leave it, even at that. "But that could not be either," he said. "For surely, if the children were being taken away to be killed, the parents would fight. They would refuse to work. And then what good would *they* be?"

Unlike Gerard, Lisette had not seen much of war or the governing of people. But she knew he was right and she didn't think she'd ever be warm again. Did Aunt Josephine or her parents suspect? Did anybody? She thought again of the family on the train — three generations: grandfather, parents, children. Had they guessed? Whispering, barely able to get the words out, *she* guessed: "They're killing them all."

18.

Wednesday, September 4, 1940 –
Thursday, September 5, 1940

When Lisette went back into the house, Cecile was waiting for her, tapping her foot impatiently. "You took long enough," she said.

"I don't feel well," Lisette said. And perhaps the truth of this showed on her face, for Cecile didn't argue. Emma, who had been holding Anne's feet while Anne tried to stand on her head on the couch, said, "What's the matter?" And Etienne stopped pretending he was an airplane, so that Louis Jerome, presumably another airplane, ran into him.

Lisette couldn't stand to look at them. "I'm going to bed," she said. She was whispering, because her head hurt. "And it's time everybody five and under went to bed, too."

"Wait," Cecile said. "Aren't you going to help?"

"No," Lisette answered. "Do it quickly and quietly and start cleaning up the mess you've made, because if you don't, I'm going to make you do it tomorrow anyway and it'll be easier if you start now."

"Bossy," Cecile called after her as she slowly climbed the stairs.

"What if she's real sick?" she heard Louis Jerome ask. "What if she dies?"

Lisette didn't wait to hear Cecile's answer. She closed the bedroom door behind her and climbed into bed fully clothed, stopping only long enough to kick off her shoes. She pulled the blanket up over her head and closed her eyes tightly and willed herself to fall asleep, but she couldn't.

The children came upstairs. Cecile and Louis Jerome were fairly well organized and more or less quiet. Emma called, "Good night" — presumably to her — but she didn't answer.

Cecile opened the bedroom door and whispered, "Are you awake, Lisette?"

Lisette pretended she wasn't.

Cecile changed into her nightgown by the light of the hallway so she didn't have to turn on the bedroom light, which was more consideration than Lisette would have expected, especially since Lisette still had her head under the covers. When Cecile climbed into bed, Lisette turned her back on her.

"Good night, Lisette," Cecile whispered.

Lisette bit her lip and didn't answer that either.

She did finally fall asleep. It seemed like hours, but Cecile had no clock in her room, so Lisette had no idea how long it really was. And when she woke up again, she couldn't tell if she'd slept for five minutes or five hours. Cecile was still asleep.

Lisette climbed out of bed and peeled back the corner of the blackout curtain. The edge of the sky was just beginning to turn from gray to pink. At least it had finally stopped raining.

Without Aunt Josephine to rouse them, there was no telling how late everybody would sleep. At least another couple of hours, she estimated.

She washed her hands and face, which made her feel better as long as she didn't think about what she had learned last night.

The electricity had gone off sometime during the night, but the gas was still on, so Lisette was able to heat water on the stove. While she waited for it to boil, she went into Uncle Raymond's study, where she found a book called *Chivalry in the Middle Ages*, which she brought back into the kitchen. She got out the coffee maker and spooned in some of the roasted acorn grounds Aunt Josephine had bought yesterday. It didn't smell half bad, and when it was ready, she poured it out into two mugs. She put the mugs on a cookie sheet, along with some more bread and several clusters of grapes and the book, and carried it all out to the barn.

She braced herself for Gerard's not being there, but he was lying on the floor, his head resting on Softy's side, in the shaft of light from the door she'd just opened. For one awful second — she *must* stop listening to Louis Jerome — she had the impression he was dead, or, at least, more dead than usual.

In the same instant she realized that his chest was moving up and down, Softy awoke and scrambled to her feet. Gerard's head hit the barn floor with a very solid *thump*.

He went from sound asleep to alert-to-danger faster than she would have believed possible. He got his feet under him and went into a defensive crouch, his hand going to his side — for his sword, she knew instinctively. Thank goodness he hadn't had one at this age or he might have taken her head off before he'd realized his mistake.

She kept forgetting that, despite appearances, he was a twenty-seven-year-old knight.

"Good morning," she said, putting down the tray.

"Good morning," he answered. She also wouldn't have thought it possible that he could blush, but she could see the embarrassed flush creeping over his cheeks.

She also kept forgetting that, despite appearances, he'd been dead for the past six hundred years.

"I thought you might not come back," he told her.

She hadn't stopped to wonder what he might think. She had been so upset last night she had run out of the barn and into the house, and of course Gerard had not dared follow nor call after her.

Lisette shook her head. "All you did was point out what I should have already seen. It does no good to be angry at you. That's like killing the bearer of bad news."

From his look, he didn't understand her reference.

She explained, "The story about the king who killed the messenger for bringing the news that they'd lost the battle?"

He shook his head, although she was fairly certain the story was from Greek or Roman times, long before the 1300s.

She shrugged to indicate it wasn't important. She sat down and patted the ground next to her. "Was your king the kind of man to kill someone for bringing bad news?"

"Yes," Gerard said so simply that there was no response she could give. He sat where she'd indicated.

"Who was he?" she asked.

"Philippe," he told her, "the Fourth."

The name meant nothing to her. She was most familiar with the kings starting from Louis XIII, which she knew was much too late. She picked up the book and found Philippe in the index. As she flipped to the appropriate section, she was aware of Gerard watching her with what was probably the same expression people had worn when Joan of Arc said she was hearing voices. "Here he is." There was even a portrait of him, wearing a silly hat. She put the book down between them. "Is it a good likeness?" she asked.

Gerard looked at her helplessly.

"Didn't you ever meet him?" she asked.

"Have you met your king?" he countered.

She didn't want to get started with that again.

"Actually, we don't have a king anymore," she admitted, then added hastily: "But even if we did, I'm not anybody important. I thought knights had to pledge loyalty to the king."

She thought he was still stuck on "We don't have a king anymore," but after a moment he said, "Not the religious orders. We answered to the pope."

"Look," Lisette said, "here it says he reigned from 1285 until —"

She stopped abruptly and Gerard looked up from her finger, pointing in the book, to her face. Apparently he couldn't read numbers either.

"Thirteen fourteen," she finished. The same year Gerard had died.

Gerard raised his eyebrows, surprised but obviously not overwhelmed. She had asked if his king was the kind of man to kill someone for bringing bad news and Gerard had answered yes. That wasn't the kind of person you mourned for. But he *had* been surprised, which indicated Gerard had died first. Many people must have died in 1314. There didn't have to be a connection.

"Let's see . . ." She ran her finger down the text.

"It talks about a war with Edward I of England, and a revolt in Flanders . . ."

"My older brother was killed fighting the Flemish," Gerard said.

Again, she had no idea how to answer. "It mentions several popes here," Lisette said. "Celestine V, pressured by Philippe to resign, replaced by Boniface VIII. Listen to this: Boniface threatened to excommunicate Philippe, but there was an uprising, possibly backed by Philippe, and Boniface died. He was followed by Benedict XI, who was poisoned, also possibly Philippe's doing, then after Benedict there was Clement V, who" — she looked up at Gerard — "died in 1314."

No reaction this time. "Does your book speak of us?" he asked.

Lisette silently skimmed more of the text. "'The Templars, who fought so bravely in the Crusades, were disbanded in dishonor in 1314,'" she read out loud — 1314 yet again — "'on what is now generally thought to have been trumped-up charges.'"

Gerard crossed his arms and sat back, his look hard and angry.

She quickly looked away. "It says Philippe confiscated what the book calls their 'considerable properties,' which were supposed to go to the Knights Hospitallers. But Philippe claimed the money was owed him because of the expenses of the Templars' trial, and he never handed it over. Do you know anything about a trial?"

"Yes," Gerard said. "Is that all?"

"No, it says he also seized property from the Lombard bankers, whoever they were, and — listen to this — from the Jews. In 1306 he deported all the Jews and said anybody who owed anything to a Jewish person had to pay the debt to *him*. It also says he debased and inflated the coinage, so that if he owed somebody money he'd say it was worth one thing, but if somebody owed him, he'd say it was worth less so they had to pay him more. Did you know that?"

"I was in Cyprus in 1306," Gerard said. "Does your book say nothing else of the Templars?"

Lisette looked up Templars in the index. "Let's see. Founded in 1118, one of several —"

Gerard sighed. Loudly.

Lisette went to one of the later pages cited in the index. "'A Crusader's Castle,'" she read, underneath a picture of a grim-looking fortress. "'Krak des Chevaliers.' Were you there?"

"I was never in the Holy Land," Gerard said.

Lisette skipped forward some more. "'The fall of Acre'?"

He shook his head.

"All that's left is that little bit about Philippe disbanding them."

Gerard rested his head in his hands.

"What *did* happen?" she asked.

He let his hands drop but said nothing.

His entire life, Lisette thought, *between where one sentence ends and the next starts.*

But there was more to it than that, she suspected.

"Tell me about yourself," she said.

"To what purpose?" He sounded tired and bitter.

"Tell me," she repeated.

19.

"All my life I trained to be a knight," Gerard said. "And in my heart I always knew I wanted to be a Templar, to dedicate myself, body and soul, to God."

"Did you have to make vows?" Lisette asked. "Like a priest?"

Gerard nodded. "Obedience, chastity, and poverty. My brother had died by then, and my father. I turned over all my family property, all my possessions to the Order."

He was speaking slowly enough, hesitantly enough that it didn't feel like interrupting to ask, "Were you rich before that?"

"Yes," Gerard said simply. "By the time I took my vows, Jerusalem had been lost." He gestured vaguely

159

toward the book on chivalry. "The fall of Acre." He shook his head. "But we always thought we'd win it back — eventually. Always."

Like us, she thought. *Like us when Germany invaded France.*

She saw him pull himself back together. "I joined the Templars in Cyprus, where we were fighting the Turks. Philippe . . . was not a popular king."

"I should think not," Lisette said.

"There was a riot in Paris, and he took refuge for several days in the Paris Temple, our headquarters. We guessed, later —" Something about that thought made him wince. He ran his hands through his hair. "Understand, the individual Templars took a vow of poverty," he told her. "But the Order itself was very rich."

"'Considerable properties,'" Lisette quoted from the book.

Gerard nodded. "The King must have seen just how rich we were while he was the guest of the Paris chapter. Can you imagine them, trying to impress him, letting him see everything, thinking that if they showed him how rich and powerful we were, he'd leave us alone?"

Lisette looked down at her hands on the book, away from the bitterness on Gerard's face.

"Within the year," he said, "Pope Clement called us back from Cyprus to meet with King Philippe, to discuss another Crusade. I was young, a new knight, a nobody. It wasn't until afterwards that I learned there were already those who suspected he'd move against us. But nobody suspected . . ." He closed his eyes.

Lisette waited.

"We returned to Paris. Everything seemed normal. Jacques de Molay, the Grand Master of our Order, was a pallbearer at the funeral for the King's brother's wife. The next day — the very day following the funeral — we were arrested."

"Who?" Lisette started to ask, at the same moment Gerard said, "All of us."

"*All?*" Lisette asked. "How many —"

"Thousands. Of course," he told her, "not all the brothers were knights. There were *confratres* —"

"What are *confratres?*"

He paused to consider. "What you called regular soldiers."

"Go on," she told him.

"Chaplains, retainers, old men and boys who were shepherds and farm laborers for the Order and who had never been to the Holy Land or to Cyprus or anywhere besides the fief to which they'd been born." He put his hands together, almost as though he was praying. When he spoke again, his voice was very soft. "They came at night, and those of us at the Paris Temple had no idea how widespread the arrests were. Our leaders ordered us not to fight, to lay down our weapons. They thought that everything would be resolved shortly if we didn't resist."

"But Philippe disbanded the Order anyway?" Lisette said.

Gerard looked at her over his clasped hands.

No, she realized. No, it hadn't been that easy.

"We were accused . . ." He sighed, lowering his gaze. "They . . ." He put his hands down on his knees and looked at them rather than at her. He opened his mouth to start again, but again changed his mind.

"You didn't do it," Lisette said, to show she believed in him.

"No," he said. And the look of appreciation and relief nearly broke her heart. "We were rich and we were arrogant, and we weren't nearly as powerful as we thought; that was all we were guilty of."

"What did they say?" she asked.

He had a hard time getting it out: "Treason — selling the Holy Land to the Saracens."

He was concentrating on his hands again so that she suspected there was more to it than that. "Yes?"

"Heresy. Denying Christ. Spitting on the cross. Idol worship." He stole a quick glance at her that told her even that wasn't the worst of it.

"Go on."

He forced himself to meet her eyes. "Immorality."

Now she looked away, but then she realized that suggested she didn't trust in his innocence. She turned back to face him. "Those are stupid accusations," she said. "Hundreds of Templars died in the Crusades."

"Thousands, over the years," he corrected her.

"Why would Saracen sympathizers or people who

didn't believe in Jesus die in His name? What evidence did they have for any of it?"

"Evidence?" Gerard pondered until Lisette wondered if the word hadn't existed in medieval times. "There were confessions," he said. Again he ran his hands over his face. He must have realized how frustrating it was for her to get his story piecemeal like this. "The Dominicans were in charge of the inquisition," he said. "The hounds of the Lord."

"Dominican *monks*?" Lisette asked. "Inquisition" made her think of torture and death, and Dominicans taught in schools.

But Gerard was nodding. "By law," he explained, "torture can be used on a person only once. If he does not confess, that means God has given him the strength to withstand the pain, which proves that he is innocent."

"I see," Lisette said, though it sounded like a roundabout way of seeking justice to her.

"But," Gerard continued, "the law does not stipulate what 'once' means."

"Once means once," Lisette said.

But Gerard said, "Once can be broken into many intervals."

"How many?"

Gerard shrugged. "Until you say whatever it is that they want you to say." He leaned forward, elbows resting on knees, head resting on his once-again clasped hands. "At first you think you'll be brave, like the heroes in the ballads. But that doesn't last long. And then you think you can't take it anymore, and surely if God won't stop them, at least He'll stop your heart and take you home to Him. And you can't stop screaming and you can't catch your breath and finally it all goes away, but then they throw a bucket of water on you and you haven't died at all, and they start all over again. Those first few days, we kept waiting for Jacques de Molay and the other leaders to do something, to get us out of there somehow. Then we heard that Molay had confessed. He was an old man. But, we said to ourselves, we're under the authority of the pope. The pope will protest, he'll demand our release. But the pope was afraid of the king. And finally he handed us over to Philippe for the greater good of the Church."

Lisette would have given anything to be able to hug him, to console him. "How long?" she asked.

"Seven years," Gerard answered, his voice a whisper. "At first I thought, I'm young but not too young. I'm innocent. I can resist. But they kept coming back and coming back. We were chained together in groups, sometimes five or six; some cells held twenty or thirty. And it was always cold and filthy, and we were always hungry, and they refused us the sacraments. And you could hear them coming, and you'd pray: Not today. God spare me today. Let them take somebody else, anybody else, one of the boys, one of the old men, my best friend. Just don't let them touch me. And then they'd tell us, 'Admit to the charges. Everybody else has. And then we can stop hurting you. This one or that one has admitted that at the receptions he presided over, the initiates were required to spit on the cross and pray to an idol. We know you were there. You don't have to give us any names, just say yes.' And after long enough, it seemed as though lying and saying yes was the only reasonable thing to do."

He'd wrapped his arms around himself and was sitting hunched over as though to protect himself. Lisette said, "Oh, Gerard, I'm so sorry. Wasn't there anybody to speak up for the Templars?"

"The third year," Gerard said, "Pope Clement ordered a papal commission to investigate. They asked, 'Who among you will defend the Order?' At first, nobody would. Nobody wanted to be noticed. But they said, 'We will protect you from retaliation. Speak freely. Speak the truth. No harm will come to you.' So we stepped forward, over five hundred of us. The commissioners put five men in charge: Pierre de Bologna and Renaud de Provins, who were priests; Guillaume de Chambonnet and Bertrand de Sartiges, knights; and Robert Vigier, a serving brother."

Gerard gave the faintest of smiles. "Renaud was a lawyer at heart. If anybody could have done anything for us . . . He said that we should be held in custody by the Church rather than by the civil authorities. He tried to ensure security for witnesses, both Templars and outsiders who would testify on our behalf. He demanded an inquiry into deathbed confessions, where many had recanted their earlier confessions of the charges against us. He said that those who accused us should appear before the commission, and that when the brothers were being examined by the commission, the king's agents should not be present."

All reasonable requests, Lisette thought. "What happened?"

"Several of the commissioners refused to attend the hearings; perhaps they were afraid, perhaps loyal to the king, I don't know why. Still, we gave our testimony. Lisette, sometimes somebody would speak in the morning, maintaining his innocence, then the same person would be brought back that afternoon or the next day, and suddenly his hands were bloodied and bandaged, or he couldn't even walk but was dragged in by the jailers, spitting blood or moaning in pain, and he'd say, 'Oh, I misunderstood the question. Yes, I did all those things.'"

"Couldn't anybody see —"

"They could see," Gerard said. "They could see. Sympathizers spread the word. In other lands — England, Scotland, Aragon — there were no confessions. Just in France. And in France, while the hearings were still going on, they loaded onto carts fifty-four of the men who had come forward to speak, and they took them outside Paris, where they burned them as relapsed heretics."

"Was that the end of the papal commission?"

"No. All in all it went on for more than two years. There were still some who spoke out, who said, 'I may eventually deny this, but that will be because of pain or fear: the Templars are innocent.' There were more burnings. Renaud de Provins was scheduled to die, but the commissioners demanded his return, since he was one of the leaders of the defense. Pierre de Bologna disappeared. They said he escaped." Gerard shook his head. "I don't know; it could be. I . . . find this difficult to believe. Brothers who had offered to defend the Order renounced that offer." He was biting his lip. "I was one of those."

"Gerard —" Lisette started.

"The commission adjourned for six months. When it reconvened, more commissioners refused to attend. Pierre was gone, whether escaped or dead, and Renaud was prohibited from attending the hearings because the Archbishop of Sens — who was a friend of the king, who had been appointed by the king — had degraded him from priesthood. Sir Guillaume and Sir Bertrand asked to be excused because they were unlettered men who didn't know the law, and I'm afraid I never quite noticed when Robert Vigier stopped attending, but it was much earlier." Gerard took a deep breath. "Eventually, the pope called an assembly. He announced that the Order could not be convicted on the evidence —"

Lisette gave a start, surprised.

" — but that he was personally convinced of our guilt. Those who had confessed and who had not renounced their confessions were released. Anyone who had refused to confess or who had retracted his confession was condemned to perpetual imprisonment."

"There were some who hadn't confessed?" Lisette asked. "Despite the torture?" And something about his expression made her ask, though she had thought earlier that he must have given in, "Were you one of them?"

"Yes," he said, barely loud enough to hear. "Eventually Jacques de Molay realized the pope would not defend us. Eventually he admitted that he had lied in confessing because of the torture. They burned him the next day. One of the jailers told us that Molay proclaimed his innocence even as the flames consumed him, that he called Philippe and Clement to meet him before God for judgment."

So that was why Gerard hadn't been surprised to hear that they'd all died the same year.

Lisette closed the book. She wanted to know what had happened to Gerard but couldn't bring herself to ask.

Perhaps he could tell. Or perhaps it was just the logical end to his story. "I died in jail of my injuries," he said, in a voice that sounded much less emotional than when he had been describing the hearings.

"Without confessing," Lisette finished for him. Surely that counted for something.

"I should have confessed," Gerard said. "I accomplished nothing." And then the calm and flat voice was shown to be false for he buried his face in his hands and his shoulders began to shake.

Instinctively Lisette threw her arms around him and she rocked him back and forth the way her mother used to do for her when she'd fallen or been upset. "It's all right," she murmured. "It's all over now," which had to be the stupidest thing in the world you could say to a ghost.

But then she realized that she was actually holding Gerard, that she could feel him in her arms and his hot tears on her neck.

20.

Thursday, September 5, 1940

"Gerard," Lisette whispered, afraid to break the spell by speaking out loud. "Gerard." She took his hand, the hand that several times had passed through her like a shiver, and twined her fingers about his.

Slowly he raised his head. He looked from their clasped hands to her face.

She put her other hand against his chest. Halfway between a laugh and a sob of relief, she asked, "Can you feel it?" But lest he think she meant only could he feel her hand, she took his free hand and placed it where hers had been. "Can you feel your heart beating?"

170

He took a deep, shuddering breath. Then he pulled his hands free of hers, but only to throw his arms around her and hold her close. She was afraid she was going to start to cry, and she bit down hard on her lip to prevent it.

That was when she heard a noise from outside that sounded like someone was crying.

Gerard heard it, too. He was already loosening his grip on her when Lisette heard Cecile calling: "Lisette! Lisette!" It wasn't whining; it wasn't anger. *She woke up and couldn't find me,* Lisette thought. *She's frightened.* In fact, Cecile must have been looking for her outside, for her voice wasn't even coming from the direction of the house, but from across the lawn. "Lisette!"

Even still in the barn, with Gerard helping her to her feet, Lisette could hear Cecile's great ragged breaths as she returned, running, from wherever she'd been looking.

"Lisette!" Cecile sobbed.

What could have happened? Lisette wondered, and thought immediately of Louis Jerome, spreading panic. She opened her mouth to say "I'm here." But before she had a chance, Cecile screamed: "Germans!"

"Cecile!" Lisette shouted. She ran to the open doorway and saw Cecile poised with her hand on the porch door. From within the house there was a commotion, the sound of little feet running. One look at

Cecile's frantic face was enough to convince Lisette of her sincerity.

"They're at Maurice's house," Cecile gasped. "They're coming."

Lisette glanced in that direction, but from this angle the wooded hill stood in the way.

"They're coming!" Cecile screamed at her before doubling over with great racking coughs.

"Easy," Gerard said.

Lisette hadn't even been aware of his coming out behind her. She gasped, remembering their question that had never been answered: What if two people of two different ages saw him at once? For the moment Cecile wasn't seeing him; her eyes were wild and unfocused, and he still looked thirteen. *Run,* Lisette wanted to warn him. *Hide.*

"Easy," Gerard said again. He took Cecile by the arm. If Lisette had realized what he was about to do, she would have warned him against that, too. But he took her by the arm, and his hand did not pass through. However, it had happened, he was well and truly there, and as solid as they. He drew Cecile in close the way Lisette had done with him. "Easy." The way he might have calmed a skittish horse.

Cecile took a deep breath. She was either going to howl hysterically or be all right. She looked right up at him. "Who are you?" she demanded.

"Gerard d'Arveyres."

Lisette was watching him, and there was not a flicker of change. Could it be, maybe, that she and

Cecile each saw him at her own age? But that was unlikely. Cecile had her head tipped back to look him in the face. Whatever it was that had caused him to come back to life — whether it was her summoning him that first day or talking to him day after day, or caring about him, or whether it was nothing at all to do with her but something about the alignment of the stars or whatever it was, he seemed to have settled into a thirteen-year-old form.

Either the fact that he was so much taller than Cecile or that Lisette had not gasped and fainted must have let him know that his body wasn't going through any strange changes. "How far away does this Maurice live?" he asked.

"One house away," Lisette said, pointing. "If Cecile took the shortcut through the fields and they're in cars on the road, they're about two minutes behind her." He didn't know about minutes. How could she rephrase that to let him see how little time there was?

But Cecile was shaking her head. "No," — she was still panting from her run — "they radioed for help."

If that meant from Sibourne, that gave them about fifteen to twenty minutes. "What happened?" Lisette demanded.

"We couldn't find you. We looked all over the house and then I thought you'd probably gone up that hill the way you keep doing."

Lisette spared a quick glance for Gerard.

Cecile said, "But I thought how you were sick last night and I was worried, so I went to Maurice's place for help. But when I got there, there was a car in the driveway with a German soldier sitting in the driver's seat. I could tell he was only the driver, because he was just sitting there filing his nails, which meant that he was waiting for something or somebody, so I sneaked around the side and got between the bushes under the window and I peeked in."

"Cecile!" Lisette gasped. "You should have come right back here."

Cecile started crying.

"Did they see you?" Lisette asked.

But that must not have been it, for Cecile was shaking her head. "It was those two officers from town who kept whistling at Maman and following her around. They were bothering us the day I went to town with her, and she said they'd been doing it before, too. Today they were standing on the upstairs landing yelling at Maurice and his wife. They must have pulled them right out of their beds because they were still in their nightclothes. The soldiers were saying that Maman was always buying too much food and who was she buying it for? Maurice said that she sometimes shopped for them, since Madame Maurice is in a wheelchair and can't get around, and that Maman always has nieces and nephews staying with her for a week or so at a time. But they didn't believe him. They said that she must be keeping Jews. Maurice said no, she wasn't. And then . . ." She was taking gulping breaths of air again.

Very gently, Gerard said, "And then . . ."

"Then they moved Madame Maurice's wheelchair right to the edge of the stairs. And they said, 'Is she keeping Jews?' Lisette, they were going to push her off! Maurice begged them not to and they kept asking, 'Is she keeping Jews?' and finally he said he didn't know, maybe. And they said, 'If she's keeping Jews, where would they be?' And they pushed the chair so that it was half off the top stair and if they let go, it would fall. And Maurice said that many of the old houses have a secret room in the basement."

Lisette gave a cry of frustration.

Gerard was watching her.

"They'll find them," Lisette said, remembering what she'd guessed last night, about the work camps. It wasn't fair that her parents were in Paris and Aunt Josephine was with Uncle Raymond and that *she* was the one left in charge. "If they know to look in the basement, they'll find them."

"But there isn't anyplace else to hide them," Cecile said.

"The caves," Gerard said.

"What caves?" Lisette and Cecile asked simultaneously.

Gerard pointed to where the little wooded hill met the limestone cliff beyond. "My brother and I spent a great deal of time exploring when we were growing up."

There was no time for further questions.

Lisette ran into the house and got the flashlight from under the sink. Gerard took a step back from her and made a sign of the cross when she flipped the switch, but she didn't have time to worry about that. "Long live France!" she started shouting as she raced down the stairs.

The children must have been frightened by her shouts, or by the sounds of Gerard and Cecile thundering down the stairs behind her.

"Long live France!" she yelled, pounding on the door. "Get out of there now. The Germans are coming and they know where to look."

The door opened a crack and Lisette used her hand to push it open all the way. "Move," she commanded. "Gerard knows where you can hide."

Anne was whimpering. Rachel, perhaps feeling the tension from her brother's arms, had begun crying. They looked at Gerard with big, frightened eyes.

And Gerard was looking at the gas mask covering Etienne's face with much the same expression.

Not now, she thought. "It's science, not magic," she told him. Then, to the children, again: "Move!"

Finally the words seemed to sink in. But in the seconds it took them to file out, while Lisette pointed her flashlight into the room behind them, she realized this plan wouldn't work.

"Wait," she said.

Cecile looked ready to panic again. "What?"

Lisette indicated the blackout drapes carefully tacked onto the walls. "If they find this room, they'll know."

"So what," Cecile demanded, "if we're in the caves?"

"So they'll wait for us to come back. And your mother will walk right into the middle of it, never suspecting."

Gerard was touching the drapes as though he'd never seen or felt anything like them. Which he probably hadn't. "Can we take this down?" he asked.

"Not easily," Cecile said. "It took my mother two days to get it up."

Louis Jerome said, "What if —"

"Louis Jerome!" Lisette shouted at him.

He cringed, but finished his thought. "What if we make it look like something else? Bring some jars of fruit in here . . . ?"

"But they'll be suspicious of the curtains," Lisette said. "Why would . . ." She stopped at the thought: Why would anybody want a room that was totally dark?

"What?" Gerard asked.

"You bring the children up the hill," she told him. "I'll meet you there and you can show us where the caves are."

"What will you be doing?"

"Making this room look like a darkroom. Never mind, there's no time to explain. Believe me, it will work."

"It's too dangerous," he said. "What if the Germans come while you're still here?"

She knew that. And if she thought about it, she wouldn't be able to move at all. "I can do this faster if the little ones are out of the way. Take them to the hill. I'll join you there."

Gerard hesitated, then he nodded.

She was about to tell him that if she were delayed, they should go on to the caves without her. But that made her think of what it was that would be happening if she *were* delayed, and that made it hard not to leave right then and there with them, which would be the end of Aunt Josephine, and besides, if she hinted that something might happen to her, she had the feeling Gerard just might pick her up and drag her away, which, again, would be the end of Aunt Josephine. "Go," she said. "I'll join you."

And to show that she knew what she was doing, she ran up the stairs ahead of them. She heard them heading for the back door as she went down the hall to Uncle Raymond's study.

A false start already, she thought, as she shifted the flashlight to her left hand. The first thing she should have done was see to getting a light so that she could use both hands. But for now she grabbed up both his cameras, hanging the one with the strap around her neck and carrying the larger one. She managed to tuck a box of photographic paper under her arm and held the red cloth for the light between her teeth.

Back downstairs, she left the photographic equipment in the secret room then went to Uncle Raymond's work area. She had to climb onto the workbench to reach the utility light, but it was worth it, for the extension cord reached all the way back. She hung it on the edge of the one shelf Aunt Josephine had left up, the one where she kept the blankets. Then she started loading the shelf with what she'd brought.

Two more trips and she had everything. She turned off the light, draped the red cloth around it, and picked up the blankets and diaper and water bottle. She left the door open so nobody would notice there was no handle.

The blankets and diaper she stuffed into the chest of out-of-season clothes, and the water she put into the kitchen cupboard. She ran back into the study to rearrange a few of the pictures of Cecile so there wouldn't be an empty space.

Had the children made the beds? Lisette hoped so. She had never found the story that she and Cecile had been playing convincing. but her heart was beating so hard it hurt, and she couldn't bring herself to stay any longer. At least there were no dishes in the sink.

Taking the flashlight with her, she ran outside and nearly tripped over Softy, who was bleating insistently and obviously needed to be milked.

"Later," Lisette promised.

Someone had taken the time to close the barn door. Gerard, she realized. All he'd had on his feet had been Uncle Raymond's socks and he would have gone back to get his boots before heading off for the woods and the caves.

She looked up the hill. Of course they'd had more than enough time to make the climb, and they'd know better than to stay at the edge where they could be seen.

Still, she hesitated at the barn, wondering if Gerard had hidden the rest of his clothes and, if not, what the Germans would make of his fourteenth-century outfit. Should she —

But she heard a low, familiar rumbling: a car engine.

Lisette ran.

21.

Thursday, September 5, 1940

At the top of the hill, Lisette looked back. Two cars with red and black swastikas were in the driveway and seven German soldiers were standing by the back door. Four of them were facing her direction, but she couldn't tell for sure if they'd seen her.

Stop being an idiot, she told herself. Of course they'd seen. At least they hadn't shot at her. Yet. She ran in among the trees before they changed their minds.

A hand grabbed her arm near the elbow, and she nearly jumped out of her skin. The hand moved to cover her mouth, but after her startled squeal, she'd already recognized Gerard.

She pulled his hand down. "They saw me," she

hissed at him so the others — just beyond him — couldn't hear. All she needed was for them to panic again. At least Rachel had stopped crying and was only fussing.

Gerard gave a quick nod to indicate he'd heard, but he didn't answer. He just gestured for everyone to follow.

They came out of the woods at a different place from the spot where Lisette had looked down on Maurice's house. Here there was a long, narrow crack in the face of the cliff and Gerard headed for that.

Lisette looked back the way they'd come, sure that they'd left a trail of broken branches and footprints that anyone could follow. Next to her, Louis Jerome looked back, too, and said exactly what she was thinking: "If they can see where we came through the woods, they'll know exactly where we've gone."

"There is more than just one cave," Gerard said. "You could spend days in here and not see it all."

If you had enough food, Lisette thought, but she didn't say it. She turned on her flashlight and Cecile turned on hers.

They had to walk single file, sideways, for several meters, then the crack opened up into the first cave.

"Where now?" Lisette moved her flashlight in an arc around the cave. There were several openings that looked big enough to pass through. She even shone the light on the ceiling, but just as she started to move the light back down to the floor, there was a rattle of pebbles from overhead and directly behind her.

She whirled around as something — she had the impression it was the size of a small German officer — launched itself at her face. She got her arm up just in time, and claws raked across her forearm. *That* told her what it was before her eyes could focus.

"Stupid cat!" she yelled, which was foolish, considering the circumstances.

Mimi gave her usual throaty growl, probably calling her a stupid human, and streaked away down a tunnel no bigger than herself.

Lisette's arm was bleeding, but there was no time to fuss over it.

Gerard chose a tunnel that was bigger than the one Mimi had used, but they all had to duck, except for the twins and Etienne.

The tunnel divided in two. Gerard led them down the section that was taller but narrower.

After several turns and a general impression of heading down, Lisette heard water. The next cavern they came to had a huge pool.

"The far wall," Gerard said, "comes just below the surface of the water. You can walk out about halfway or so. He glanced at the younger children skeptically. "Then we'll have to swim the rest of the way. Who knows how to swim?"

"I'm a wonderful swimmer," Cecile announced.

"Me, too," Etienne said.

Lisette judged the distance and nodded.

Louis Jerome shook his head *no.* The twins just stared at Gerard.

"All right," Gerard said. "Those of us who know how to swim will help the others."

"What happens when we get to the wall?" Lisette asked.

"It only goes about this far under the water." Gerard held his hands apart about as tall as the twins.

This was sounding worse and worse. The younger children were beginning to give each other panicked looks.

Lisette, who could swim but not very well, said, "So we have to hold our breath, dive into the water, pass under the wall . . ." Gerard was nodding. "For how long?"

"About a fifty-count."

"*Fifty?*" Even assuming counting faster than seconds, she'd never make it. "Gerard."

"I can help you," he said. "Halfway beneath the wall, the floor comes up and you can walk out to the other side. The water there . . ." He was indicating waist high. Which was still taller than the twins.

"What about the baby?" Etienne asked.

"Babies know how to hold their breath under water," Gerard said.

Cecile added, "Everybody knows that."

Lisette started to object again, but Etienne cut her off. "What about the baby?" he repeated more loudly.

"*I'll* take the baby," Gerard said. "The baby will be fine."

"You're going to kill the baby!" Etienne protested.

Gerard looked at Lisette as though expecting her

to convince Etienne. "I don't know," she started, "isn't —"

"You're going to kill the baby!" Etienne was shouting.

"Stop it," Cecile said. "The Germans will hear you."

Etienne got even louder. "You're going to kill the baby!"

Gerard stooped down in front of him and took his arm. "I would do nothing that would harm the baby," he said.

"Nobody *wants* to hurt a baby." Etienne was still shouting, but now he was crying, too. He yanked his arm away from Gerard. "My Maman didn't *want* to hurt *our* baby. Those things happen."

The last was obviously something he'd heard adults saying. The rest made no sense. Lisette stooped down also, shoulder to shoulder with Gerard. "Etienne, hush, quiet now. What are you saying?"

"When the Germans came to *my* house." He was still shouting, though not quite so loudly.

"What happened when the Germans came to your house?" Lisette asked. "Shh. Quietly now."

Etienne wiped his hand across his nose. "We hid in the attic," he said. "In the clothes chest. Me and Maman and my baby brother that we hadn't had a chance to name yet."

Lisette put her fingers to her lips and Etienne's voice dropped to a normal level. "We could hear the Germans coming up the stairs and the baby started to cry. Maman said, 'Hush, little baby; hush, little baby,' but he kept crying and the Germans kept coming, and Maman put her hand over his mouth so they couldn't hear him crying, but he kept crying and we knew the Germans would hear him, so Maman held him real tight to her" — Etienne put both hands up to his chest to show how — "and the baby *didn't* know how to hold his breath."

For a long moment they just stayed there, looking at each other, listening to Etienne cry. Then Lisette pulled him in for a hug, being careful not to hold him too tight. She could see Gerard over Etienne's head.

"We'll go another way," Gerard said.

They had to go back part of the way, to one of the other tunnels that they had passed. And as they went back, they heard the approaching sound of hobnailed boots on the stone floor.

Gerard motioned for quiet, but everybody had heard already and they were walking on tiptoes and breathing as quietly as they could. Lisette was holding Rachel, and Rachel seemed to enjoy the moving around. For the moment.

Gerard ducked into a tunnel they had to crawl through.

It was difficult to crawl while holding Rachel, but the tunnel was short, and as soon as Gerard got to the end, he turned back around to take the baby from her arms long enough so she could get through the last, narrowest bit.

Once they were all through, Gerard motioned for them to sit. He pointed at the flashlights Etienne and Louis Jerome were now holding, and the boys turned off the switches.

In the total darkness, Lisette felt that the stone walls and ceiling were closing in on her. She thought of the hugeness of the hills and she thought of all that rock collapsing on her, smothering her, crushing the air out of her till she slowly died. Or it might happen so fast she wouldn't even know it. She could be dead in less than an instant. Something touched her shoulder and she jumped, but it was only Gerard. He put his mouth to her ear and whispered, "Breathe through your nose."

She realized how loud she'd been and she put her hand over her mouth to make sure she didn't forget again. She stretched her legs out to feel the wall and sat tall so that her head touched the ceiling. Not that that would keep the stone from crushing her, but at least she would know it was coming.

And all the while there was the echoing sound of the boots, and then she could hear voices, closer and closer. She didn't understand German, but she could recognize the note of complaint in the voice that muttered constantly; and the other one — that obey-me-I'm-the-one-in-charge voice that was barking short orders: "Look here. Check there," she imagined.

The boots and the voices must be on the other side of their tunnel, but there were two sharp angles, so they couldn't see the Germans' light. Rachel started to squirm, not liking the dark and the stillness and Lisette's tight grasp.

Don't cry, Lisette mentally begged, frantically rocking her. *Please don't cry.* She imagined Etienne and his mother and his baby brother huddled in the clothes chest, except that in her mind his mother looked like *her* mother, and the baby was *her* brother, François. She leaned forward to give Rachel's face desperate, distracting kisses. *Don't cry.*

It must have taken the Germans all of five minutes to pass by and then move out of hearing, but it felt like forever.

After the last echoes of their passing had died away, Gerard whispered, "Do the lights come back on?"

There were two flares of brightness.

The walls, Lisette was happy to see, were exactly where they were supposed to be, and Rachel was contentedly sucking on a strand of Lisette's hair.

Gerard was already on his feet. "Careful," he warned. "There's a drop."

Just beyond where they had stopped, the floor ended as abruptly as though it had been cut off. Etienne pointed his flashlight over the edge.

Gerard leapt down before Lisette had a chance to see the bottom. He skidded but didn't fall on the stones underfoot. He'd jumped about twice his height. One by one, they got the children down, the older ones going last to help the smaller ones. Lisette was the very last. She sat on the edge with her legs dangling. Gerard reached up as she reached down, and she felt, all in all, that it was a fairly elegant jump. She looked into his eyes and thought what a terrible thing it would be to die at this point in her life.

Eventually, after many choices and turns and climbs and drops, with Cecile complaining that Rachel's diaper had begun to leak, Gerard called a stop. By then he was carrying Anne, and Lisette was carrying Emma, who was getting heavier with every step. They were in a small cavern through which a stream of water trickled down from a small hole in the wall, over a lip of rock so that it was a tiny waterfall at just the right height to drink from, and across the floor to disappear into a crack.

"If we hear them coming, we can continue this way," Gerard said, indicating another hole only large enough for crawling. "But I doubt they'll get this far."

"What if the flashlights burn out?" Louis Jerome asked. "How will we get back?"

"Why don't you turn yours off?" Lisette said, aware that she wasn't answering his question. "We only need one."

"What if the Germans keep looking for us and looking for us?" he asked.

"Stop asking so many questions." She closed her eyes and tried to rest.

But she couldn't get his questions out of her head.

She sat leaning her back against Gerard's, which gave her the chance to talk to him quietly, so the others couldn't hear. "They will, you know," she told him. "They'll keep looking. They know we're here. They know we have something to hide."

He nodded.

She didn't like feeling helpless. She remembered the Jewish family on the train and remembered how helpless she had felt then, and she felt just as helpless now.

"They know *I'm* here," she corrected herself. "I'm the only one they saw."

He craned his neck to look at her.

"If there was some way I could convince them that I had some good reason to be here . . ." she said. "I could say that I didn't see them at the house, that I wasn't running away from them, but just exploring the caves, me alone, by myself . . ."

"You want to go back?" Gerard asked.

"No," she admitted.

But after a while she asked, "What are good reasons for going into caves?"

Gerard sighed. "They wouldn't believe you, no matter what you said."

"Probably not," she agreed.

But then she said, "The longer I'm here, the less likely they are to believe me."

"Lisette," Gerard said.

"And the lights *will* go out," — she realized he had no way of knowing that — "they won't last the day."

190

He shook his head. "What would you do?"

She thought back to when they were first entering the caves, how she'd been startled by Mimi. "I'll tell them I was looking for my cat. That she ran away and I know she sometimes comes here."

"Lisette," Gerard said, as though this was the stupidest thing he'd ever heard. And maybe it was.

"If not," she said, "it's exactly where we were before: with them knowing and arresting Aunt Josephine when she comes back, and eventually finding us and arresting us." She didn't finish the thought: *and sending us to a work camp that doesn't exist.* "What do you think?" she asked.

Gerard sighed and wouldn't meet her eyes.

"Gerard?"

He did, at last, look directly at her. "Lisette," he said. He started again. "I died once. I don't want to die again." He shook his head. "Not after one day. I don't know if I will cease to exist when I once again reach my twenty-seventh year. But I want more than a day."

She stood and, turning around, saw that while she and Gerard had talked, all the others had gathered in and been listening.

"I'm not expecting you to come back with me," she told him, and it was true. "In fact, it would be better if you didn't; how would I explain you?"

"You're throwing your life away," he whispered.

"I should have confessed," he had told her earlier. *"I accomplished nothing."*

She couldn't ask him to do that again. "I have to

go," she told him. "I have no choice. Just bring me back to where I can find my way — or to where the Germans are."

He got up without arguing, without saying anything.

It was Lisette who had to tell the children, "We'll need both flashlights: I need to get to the entrance to the cave, and Gerard will need to come back here." She didn't know if he'd really return. He probably knew a back way out. At the very least, he knew these caves well enough to circle around the Germans. And she couldn't blame him if he did; he didn't know these children, and he didn't believe they could escape the Germans. How many times could someone be expected to die for nothing?

Etienne handed her his lit flashlight then leaned over to pick up the other one.

"I'll come back to get you when the Germans are gone," she told them.

Gerard didn't correct her. He didn't say, "I'll be back before then."

Etienne turned on the second flashlight and saluted her with it before handing it to Gerard.

"I'm sorry you'll have to wait in the dark," she said, remembering how afraid she'd been when they'd been without light for that short while. But she owed Gerard at least a chance.

"Don't go," Emma said, the only one to say anything.

"It will be safer here," Lisette said. "And it

shouldn't be too long." She had a sudden mental image of her parents telling her much the same thing in much the same cheerful and perky tone. She remembered her mother, turning her face away at the last moment to tend to baby François, and Lisette knew if she had a baby to hold now, she also could have pretended to be preoccupied with it so no one would see how deeply worried she was.

Gerard led her back and back through the caves until they reached the place where he'd made that one jump and then helped them all down. Coming this way, there were indentations on the surface that made very easy handholds and footholds. Still, he clasped his hands and gave her a boost.

She scrambled up onto the higher level. Lying down to reach to help him, she heard faint voices. German voices. "I can make it from here," she whispered down to him.

He said the first thing since he'd told her, back in the cavern with the children, that she was throwing her life away. He said, "God go with you," which sounded much more final than "Good luck."

But she said, "Thank you," and headed toward where the Germans were searching for her, and she didn't look back again.

22.

The last thing she wanted, Lisette decided, was to have the Germans think she was sneaking around. So she called, tentatively at first because her voice wouldn't cooperate, but then louder, "Mimi. Here, Mimi. Here, kitty, kitty, kitty." She made cat-summoning sounds. "Here, kitty."

And suddenly there was a blaze of light right up in her face. A hand took hold of her arm roughly so that she almost dropped her own flashlight, and an angry voice demanded something of her in German.

Lisette couldn't have been more frightened, but she tried to act more confused than she really was. They must have heard her coming and had turned off their own lights until she was close enough to grab —

which, hopefully, meant that they had heard her calling the cat. "Who are you?" she asked, squinting into the lights. "Where's my cat? What have you done to my cat?"

A different voice said something that sounded just as angry as the first, but the one who was holding the flashlight closest to her eyes took a step back.

Lisette blinked the red and yellow spots away. Five soldiers — including the lieutenant who had been flirting with Aunt Josephine. But she was relieved to see that his companion, the captain who had blown kisses to *her* was not there. She remembered what Cecile had said, about how they'd threatened Madame Maurice. She tried to sound more surprised than frightened. "You're German soldiers," she said to the man who still gripped her arm.

"What are you doing here?" one of the men she didn't recognize asked in an accent so thick, it wasn't until he finished speaking that she realized it had been French. On his collar were the twin lightning bolt *S*'s that identified him as a member of the SS, the Nazi secret police.

"I'm looking for my cat," she said. "She ran away and —"

"*Schweige*," the man said, which must have meant "Quiet!" Or maybe "Liar." "Where are the others?"

She assumed he was bluffing, that he hadn't seen anybody besides her. "What others? Do you mean other cats? There's only one. Her name is Mimi and —"

The man holding her shook her. This time her flashlight did fall out of her hand. It hit the ground and the glass broke and the light went out.

"Stop this nonsense about a cat!" shouted the SS officer.

"You broke my flashlight," Lisette said. "How am I ever going to find my cat without a flashlight?"

The lieutenant she'd seen in Sibourne snorted in amusement and said something in German. The other two men grinned. "*Katze*," one of them said, a repetition of part of what the lieutenant had said. Probably "cat."

"Cats are not cave dwellers, I think," the lieutenant said. "Even in France."

The SS officer — he must be the one in charge — snapped something in German. Everything sounded angry in German, but this must have been a reprimand because it wiped the smiles off everybody's faces. "How many Jews are there?" he demanded of Lisette. "And where have you hidden them?"

"Please," Lisette said, "I don't know anything about Jews." He was going to hit her, she could tell. She cringed against the soldier holding her. "Look at my arms," she cried.

It must have sounded bizarre enough that it intrigued them. The man holding her arm twisted it so that the underside was showing, with all the scratches she'd gotten from Mimi the past several days. The ones from when Mimi had jumped on her at the cave entrance were dramatically puffy and beaded and smeared with blood.

The Sibourne lieutenant stepped forward for a closer look. He gave a low whistle. "That's some cat you have," he told her.

"She's a stray," Lisette said. "I'm trying to tame her, but she ran away. There's a dish outside our back door where we feed her — if you want, I can show you. I was trying to coax her to come into the house." To herself, she added, *Where she can lurk under tables and attack unwanted visitors.*

The SS officer said something that sounded as though it had the word "stray" in it, but she couldn't make out any of the rest of it.

The lieutenant answered, in German, which may have meant that he was translating "stray." Or they may have been discussing the likelihood of what she claimed.

The SS officer looked at her arm again. Lisette was expecting sympathy, but he grabbed her hair at the back of the neck. "We shall see," he said. "We shall see exactly what the others have discovered back at the house. You will be sorry if you're lying."

The one behind gave her a shove, and the Germans led her back the way they'd come.

They'd used stones to scratch marks on the walls and floor of the cave to keep track of where they'd been, which was a good thing because they didn't go the way Gerard had led and she lost all sense of direction after less than two minutes. If they'd asked her which way to go, they'd have quickly realized she wasn't familiar with the caves, and then they'd never believe that she'd come in here looking for a cat.

The Germans' way was more roundabout than Gerard's, but eventually they got back to where they'd started. Outside, she saw that the sun was west of center — past noon. *Don't let her be home,* she prayed, meaning Aunt Josephine. That would only complicate things. *Let the weather last night have been too bad for Uncle Raymond's drop, so that she won't come back until tomorrow.* By tomorrow, things would have settled, one way or the other.

The soldiers were neither particularly rough nor gentle with her as they went through the woods and down the hill.

"See," Lisette said, pointing to the cat's bowl by the back door.

"*Schweige,*" the one in charge said again.

There were two Germans sitting in the kitchen; one was the captain from Sibourne, the other must have been the one assigned to search through the basement room where the coal was kept, for he was filthy with black dust. They stood at attention as the group from the caves entered, which proved that the SS officer *was* in charge, but it was obvious they'd been taking it easy, their feet up on the chairs, glasses of wine in front of them. One of them — the soldier, not the captain — had been looking through a book,

Uncle Raymond's book that she'd left in the barn, *Chivalry in the Middle Ages.*

The SS officer disapproved. Lisette suspected he disapproved of everything. He yelled at the two before giving them a chance to talk. When they spoke, they gestured, indicating the house, the barn, the chrysanthemum field. Describing their search, Lisette realized.

She didn't think they'd found anything definite, for the SS officer didn't confront her with any evidence. Instead, he demanded, "Where is your mother?"

"My aunt," Lisette corrected. "She and my cousin went to visit a neighbor."

"Which neighbor?"

"I don't know."

"You *don't know?*" Obviously he didn't believe that.

"I don't live here," she explained. "I just arrived Sunday from Paris. She told me the woman's name, but I can't remember. She said she'd be back in time to prepare supper." If the Germans were still here at suppertime, it would be because they didn't believe her anyway. "It's the woman who has arthritis," Lisette said. "And the husband is either dead or blind or has bad kidneys or something."

The Germans discussed this among themselves, possibly trying to determine a name from her information.

The SS officer's tone seemed even more angry than usual.

The captain from Sibourne took hold of her arm.

"What are you doing?" Lisette said, although it was obvious what he was doing: he was bringing her to the door. "Where are you taking me?" She'd been frightened before; but, deep down, she'd thought she could convince them. "My aunt will be worried if she comes home and I'm not here."

"If your aunt returns," the SS officer said, "she will be arrested, also."

"I haven't done anything," Lisette protested.

The one holding her looked much too friendly. "Don't worry, *Fräulein*, I'll take care of you."

"*I haven't done anything,*" Lisette repeated, trying to twist away from him.

But he just tightened his grip and broadened his smile.

Two of the men were obviously staying behind — the lieutenant and one of the soldiers. The SS officer, the captain who held her, and the three other soldiers were almost at the door.

"Lisette!" a voice called from outside.

For a second, she was too frightened to recognize it.

"Lisette, I found your cat!"

Gerard, she realized, just as he opened the door. Her heart sank. He should have stayed away.

But he was triumphantly holding Mimi up by the scruff of her neck. She was hissing and spitting and had fluffed her fur out to twice her normal size so that she looked like an attack badger.

They'll never believe you, Lisette thought. *You were right. You should have stayed away.*

"What's this?" the SS officer sputtered.

"This is a cat," Gerard explained patiently. "Why are you here? Has something happened to Aunt Josephine?"

The SS officer took a step back. Lisette didn't blame him. The cat was twisting around in Gerard's grip, kicking her back feet so that the sleeve of the sweater Gerard wore was all pulled and tattered; and beyond the edge of the sleeve, his wrist was bleeding.

"Put that thing down," the SS officer demanded.

Gerard let Mimi drop.

She landed right side up, but she was not pleased. She obviously felt cornered, and made a tight circle, glaring at all the legs around her.

The SS officer took another step away from her, which was unfortunate for it put him directly by the open window and Mimi knew an escape route when she saw one. She went up his leg, across his chest, over his shoulder, and out the window, yowling and clawing him all the way.

Lisette hesitated a second, unsure whether it was overdoing her naive act to complain about her cat getting loose again.

In that second, the SS officer pulled out his pistol.

In the space of time between one heartbeat and the next, Lisette saw him raise his weapon and take aim out the window; she saw his finger tighten on the

trigger; she heard the explosion of the firing — much louder than she would have ever anticipated — and saw his arm jerk up from the recoil. The smell of gunpowder tickled her nose.

In the awful silence that followed, Lisette saw the shock on Gerard's face, as though he'd seen a weapon from hell itself, and she saw the momentary twitch of a smile on the SS officer's face; pleasure at the kill itself or at his marksmanship, she couldn't tell. Despite her ongoing feud with the cat, Lisette was grateful she wasn't in a position to see out the window. *It could be us next,* she thought. *It wouldn't make any difference to him.*

But he didn't aim the pistol at her or Gerard. He jammed it back in his holster and pulled back the sleeve of his left arm, trying to examine the damage Mimi had done. Lisette didn't have to understand German to recognize what he must be saying. Then, furiously tapping his finger against his wristwatch, he barked an order to his men in German.

The captain protested, using the word *Juden.* Jew or Jews or Jewish; she remembered the word from the German who'd pulled the family from the train. The captain must have been pointing out that Gerard might be one of the Jews they were looking for.

"Identity papers," the lieutenant demanded while the SS officer glared impatiently.

"What?" Gerard asked, knowing enough not to glance at Lisette for clarification.

"Where are your identity papers?"

Gerard considered briefly. "Aunt Josephine has them."

Which wasn't a very good response — but apparently good enough.

The SS officer grasped Gerard under the chin, roughly tipping his face for a closer look. Gerard tensed as though about to pull away, but he didn't. The German scrutinized his face. "*Nein*," he finally said, which Lisette knew meant "no." He gave Gerard a shove, then he said something that ended in "*nicht Jüdisch*." Not Jewish, she realized. The SS officer had declared that Gerard didn't look Jewish. He growled something else to his men.

Again the captain protested.

The SS officer must not have been used to captains arguing with him. "*Schweigen*, Zer!" he shouted at him. "*Lass gehen!*" From the impatient gesture he made indicating the door, *lass gehen* must mean "move." "*Lass gehen! Lass gehen!*"

Finally, the captain let go of her.

Again the Germans started to move to the door, this time all of them, this time leaving Lisette and Gerard behind.

Hardly daring to believe she was still alive, Lisette pulled out one of the kitchen chairs and sat down heavily.

Outside, two car motors started, one after the other. Tires crunched gravel. The hum of the engines faded in the direction of Sibourne.

Then, belatedly, she began to shake. "I don't know

what to do if they come back," she admitted.

From behind her, Gerard answered, "They won't. Their commander said they'd wasted a whole day already and the proof pointed more to sloppy house-keeping than Jews."

Lisette turned around to face him. "You speak German?" she asked.

"I speak Frankish," Gerard corrected her. "The Teutonic Knights certainly wouldn't lower themselves to speak French, and their Latin was so bad, it was easier just to give in and learn Frankish. This was not that much different."

Lisette leaned back in her seat. "Thank you," she said. "For coming back for me."

"It seemed to me," he said, "if you claimed to be looking for a cat, having a cat might be useful. Though it didn't work out well for the cat."

"Thank you," she repeated, not willing to let him make light of what he'd done.

He nodded to acknowledge that he understood.

"Let's get the children," she said.

23.

Once they found the children, frightened but un-harmed, Lisette cried over each of them, though she had promised herself she wouldn't, and she kissed them all. Even Cecile. Even Louis Jerome, who made a face. Etienne had given his gas mask to Anne, "So she won't be so afraid of everything," he explained, and Lisette kissed him twice.

She thought all the emotion had been wrung out of her, but as they crossed the backyard and were almost to the house she saw a movement on the porch: some-one who had been sitting got to his feet, and her heart nearly stopped and then thudded wildly so that she felt the fluttering in her throat. She'd been carrying

Rachel since the bottom of the hill and she didn't think she could run far with her. And Gerard had been carrying both twins even longer: one in his arms, the other on his back, her arms clutched around his neck, so that he'd begun weaving with exhaustion.

"Don't be frightened. It's just me."

It was too dark to see, but Lisette recognized the voice. Maurice.

He opened the door for them. His face was white and his hands were shaking. "Are you all right?" he asked.

"Yes," Lisette said.

He must have been able to tell from her voice that she knew what had happened. Or he felt so guilty, he just assumed she did. "I am so sorry," he said.

She handed Rachel to Louis Jerome, and Maurice took her hand, took Cecile's hand, looked at all the others. "I am so sorry," he repeated. "They were going to hurt my wife, and she's so frail, so . . . frail. I was frightened. I'm sorry. I didn't know what to do."

"I understand," Lisette said.

"I have never willingly hurt anyone," Maurice told them.

Emma tugged on his sleeve. "You gave us the goat," she said.

For a moment he just looked down at her, as though unable to understand what she was saying.

"Softy," Anne said, peeking shyly from around Gerard's leg. The gas mask hung down her back, held by the chin strap around her neck.

"We named the goat Softy," Emma explained.

Then Maurice did understand. His eyes filled with tears and he cupped his hand under Emma's chin. He reached out his other hand to Anne, who ducked shyly back behind Gerard's leg.

"Sometimes," Gerard said, "there's nothing we *can* do. Sometimes there are no right choices and we have to trust that God knows our intentions."

Maurice nodded slowly. "Thank you." He moved to leave, resting his hand briefly on Gerard's arm.

But then he stopped at the door and looked back at Gerard. "Do I know you?" he asked.

Straight-faced, Gerard answered, "My family has lived here for years."

Maurice nodded again, slowly, and left.

Lisette sat on the floor, too exhausted to make it to a chair. Gerard sat behind her, back to back as they'd been in the cavern. The younger children were already recovering from their ordeal: Etienne started making airplane noises and chasing Anne; Cecile offered to brush Emma's hair, and Emma ran away squealing; Louis Jerome said, "Rachel has been in the same diaper all day. If I don't change it, she'll get a rash."

It must be almost time to get supper started, Aunt Josephine obviously wasn't going to get back until tomorrow, the cat needed to be buried, and the poor goat hadn't been milked all day, but Lisette didn't want to move. She also needed to write a letter to her parents, to tell them that she was fine and that she was enjoying her stay in Sibourne, which was nice, though quiet, and that they shouldn't worry. She worked on the wording, but didn't have the energy to get the pen and paper.

Cecile sat down cross-legged by the two of them. "I knew," she said.

"You knew what?" Lisette asked.

But Cecile was talking to Gerard. "I knew before you said it in the caves. Even if I hadn't recognized you — and I did — I certainly would have recognized my father's sweater."

"Ah," Gerard said.

"But I'm good at keeping secrets," Cecile said. "I just wanted you to know."

"Thank you," he told her.

"Will you stay?" she asked him.

"Where else would I have to go?"

"That's a terrible answer," Lisette told him.

"I don't know how much time I have been given," he said softly. "I may well die again when I reach twenty-seven years of age."

Lisette said, "*I* may well die when I reach twenty-seven."

Gerard looked at her appraisingly. Then he lifted his chin. "Yes," he said to Cecile. "I will stay. I would like nothing better than to stay. If your mother," — he nodded to include Lisette — "your Aunt Josephine will have me."

"Of course Aunt Josephine will let you stay,"

Lisette said. "We'll tell her you're a poor Gypsy boy with nowhere else to go."

From the doorway Anne and Emma giggled. "He's not a Gypsy," Emma said.

"But we could say he is," Lisette pointed out.

The girls giggled again, but nodded.

"We can use being a Gypsy as an excuse for your accent and the fact that you've never been to school," Lisette told him. "And while you're here, we can teach you twentieth-century customs."

"If he's supposed to be a Gypsy," Cecile said, "I'd better brush his hair so that he *looks* like a Gypsy."

Emma and Anne exchanged a wide-eyed look that Gerard, facing Cecile, missed.

I should probably warn him, Lisette thought. But then she decided it was probably best if he learned to cope with his new world on his own.

AUTHOR'S NOTE

Although the characters in this book are fictional, Lisette and Gerard's worlds are both based on real historical periods.

GERARD'S WORLD

In the eleventh century Europe was united by a single goal. Peasants, nobles, priests, and knights — people from various countries — all worked together. Their purpose was a holy war — a crusade — to win the Holy Land of the Bible back from the Muslims. So sure were the European Christians of the rightness of their cause that their motto was *Deus volt*, which means, "God wills it."

While today many of us think of religious people as being thoughtful and gentle, for two hundred years popes urged and actively supported holy wars. There were several brotherhoods of knights whose members were monks; the Knights Templars was one such group.

By the early fourteenth century the Crusades were over, a failure. But the orders of knights who returned home were rich and powerful — both a temptation and a potential threat to the European kings and Church hierarchy that had encouraged their formation. The events described by Gerard all happened: the arrest and imprisonment of the Templars by King Philip IV of France, Philip's use of propaganda and terrorism against his enemies so that even those opposed to his policies dared not complain, and the eventual dissolution of the Templars order. As the imprisoned Templars learned, it was safer to accept the lies, to confess and accept forgiveness.

With the exception of Gerard, the participants mentioned were actual persons.

LISETTE'S WORLD

Closer to our own time, in the 1930s and 1940s, Adolf Hitler also used relentless lies against his enemies, which included not only Jews, but Gypsies, Jehovah's Witnesses, homosexuals, and those with physical disabilities. Hitler's intent was to make people fear and despise these targets of his hate, and this — again — was coupled with ruthless suppression of any who might speak out against him. Some believed Hitler's lies; others conspired to help those he oppressed; but many were simply paralyzed by fear.

In 1940, after Germany had invaded France, the French government agreed to divide the country into two regions: the Occupied Zone to be run by the Germans, and the Unoccupied Zone under the direction of the Vichy government of France. The French government agreed to this arrangement in an attempt to stop the killing and to prevent Germany from taking control of the entire country. But some in France opposed this decision, feeling that the cost of such a peace was too high. Resistance fighters were those French men and women who continued to fight against both the Germans and anyone who collaborated with them. The actions of the Resistance were countered by brutal retaliation, often against innocent bystanders — again, governing by fear.

OUR WORLD

Looking back over history, it is easy to make judgments and label the actions of long-ago people and governments "right" or "wrong." But history, in one way or another, constantly repeats itself, and things happen that seem like echoes of events that happened before. So we must repeatedly ask ourselves would we — should we — do the same as those before us? That has always been the most difficult question for any era: Which is the better course of action: to fight for what you know is right, or to keep yourself and your loved ones safe?

RELATED READING

Barber, Malcolm. *The Trial of the Templars*. England: Cambridge University Press, 1978. A detailed look at the last seven years of the Templars, including excerpts from transcripts of the trial.

Collins, Larry, and Dominique Lapierre. *Is Paris Burning?* New York: Simon & Schuster, 1965. A history of the last days of the German occupation of France.

Greenfeld, Howard. *The Hidden Children*. Boston: Houghton Mifflin Company, 1993. True-life accounts of children who survived the Holocaust by hiding or disguising themselves.

Simon, Edith. *The Piebald Standard*. Boston: Little, Brown & Co., 1959. An overview of the Crusades, with special emphasis on the role played by the Knights Templars.